# STACEY'S SECRET FRIEND

**Other books by**
**Ann M. Martin**

*Leo the Magnificat*
*Rachel Parker, Kindergarten Show-off*
*Eleven Kids, One Summer*
*Ma and Pa Dracula*
*Yours Turly, Shirley*
*Ten Kids, No Pets*
*Slam Book*
*Just a Summer Romance*
*Missing Since Monday*
*With You and Without You*
*Me and Katie (the Pest)*
*Stage Fright*
*Inside Out*
*Bummer Summer*

THE KIDS IN MS. COLMAN'S CLASS series
BABY-SITTERS LITTLE SISTER series
THE BABY-SITTERS CLUB mysteries
THE BABY-SITTERS CLUB series
CALIFORNIA DIARIES series

# STACEY'S SECRET FRIEND

## Ann M. Martin

AN
**APPLE**
PAPERBACK

SCHOLASTIC INC.
New York Toronto London Auckland Sydney

*The author gratefully acknowledges*
*Suzanne Weyn*
*for her help in*
*preparing this manuscript.*

Cover art by Hodges Soileau



ISBN 0-590-05989-0



12 11 10 9 8 7 6 5 4 3 2 1 7 8 9/9 0 1 2/0

Printed in the U.S.A. 40

First Scholastic printing, September 1997

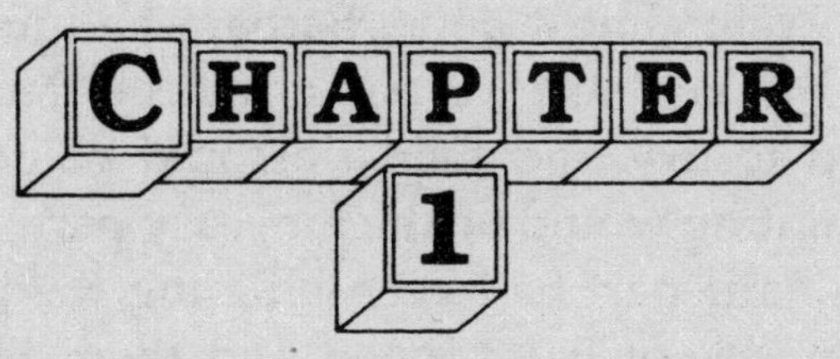


I stared into a pair of intense green eyes. They stared back at me, their gaze fixed and unwavering — kind of spooky. "Cool," I said.

"Definitely cool," agreed Barbara Hirsch, nodding thoughtfully. "Stacey, the eyes are awesome."

We were outside the back door of Stoneybrook Middle School (SMS), putting the finishing touches on a papier-mâché jaguar. We'd received permission to work there during our study hall.

The September afternoon was a little chilly, as it often is here in Connecticut this time of year, but we didn't mind. We were hoping the gooey paper strips would dry faster in the light breeze.

The jaguar is our school mascot. Barbara and I are on the SMS Pep Squad, and we'd built the jaguar in preparation for the school's first big football game of the season. The Pep Squad members would carry him onto the field during halftime.

Barbara and I had been working on him every day after school, and he was finally done. Well, almost done. Barbara had just applied the last strip of papier-mâché. Now he needed to dry, and then we could paint him. But painting would be the fun, easy part.

The hard part had been building the jaguar from pieces of balsa wood and then draping the goo-soaked papier-mâché strips over him. He was big, about the size of a kid. If Claudia hadn't helped, I don't think we could have done it.

Claudia Kishi is my best friend and a super-talented artist. She isn't on the Pep Squad, but she can't resist an art project that cries out for her touch. She'd helped us with the construction of the frame, and it had been her idea to stick large green marbles in the head for eyes.

That's what I had just finished doing. I'd pushed the marbles into the jaguar's wet papier-mâché head. As the stuff hardened, it would hold the marbles in place. At least, I hoped it would.

We heard the last buzzer of the day. "I can't stay much longer," I told Barbara. "I have a BSC meeting today." BSC stands for Baby-sitters Club. It's one of the most important things in my life, but I'll tell you more about it later.

"Okay," Barbara replied as she smoothed a bump in the jaguar's long tail. "Let's just let him dry a few more minutes, then we'll carry him back to the art room. We'll have to be careful, though. He's still so fragile. Maybe we could slide him onto a piece of cardboard. I'll go see if one of the custodians can help me find a big box." But Barbara didn't leave. She stood there admiring our marvelous creation.

We could hear lockers slamming inside. Buses were pulling into the parking lot. Kids began running out the back door.

Working with Barbara had been fun. It was the first time I'd seen her show real enthusiasm about anything in awhile. Not long ago, Barbara's best friend, Amelia Freeman, was killed by a drunk driver. Barbara had been devastated. Lately, though, she seemed to be pulling out of her depression. She'd thrown herself into this fall's Pep Squad activities, especially into making the jaguar.

I was smiling to myself, admiring the jaguar and thinking about the change in Barbara. I glanced up just in time to see a girl about to walk right into the jaguar.

"No!" I yelled.

"Stop!" Barbara shouted.

Too late. The girl's foot smashed into his mushy rib cage.

"Oh my gosh!" she cried, startled. "Oh, no! Yuck!"

I cringed as her black boot shot through to the other side.

"I'm so sorry," she said as she hopped backward, the jaguar still stuck to her foot. She managed to push it off, but she lost her balance. Barbara grabbed her from behind, to keep her from falling backward. But that sent the girl toppling forward. Her hands shot out to protect herself as she fell — onto the jaguar. By the time she hit the ground, her hand was buried in the jaguar's back.

Pulling her hand out, she looked up at Barbara and me, red-faced. "Sorry," she said in a small, embarrassed voice. "I didn't see him."

I wanted to cry. Our beautiful jaguar was ruined. It was hard to believe that something that had taken days to construct could be wrecked in mere seconds.

But after all, it had been an accident. I felt sorry for the girl. She obviously felt bad, and she looked funny too, sitting there covered in papier-mâché glop.

I glanced at Barbara for her reaction. She simply looked stunned. Her jaw was open and her eyes were wide, as if she couldn't believe what had just happened. Then she pulled herself together and extended a hand to the girl to help her up. "Are you okay?" she asked.

"Fine, if you don't count being so embarrassed and sorry I want to disappear off the planet," the girl replied glumly as she took Barbara's hand. She had a slightly odd way of speaking. It wasn't an accent exactly, but she stretched the words out in an unusual singsong.

I knew she was new in school and new to Stoneybrook, but I didn't know her name or where she'd come from.

I plucked a pair of black-rimmed glasses from the grass and handed them to her. "Thanks," she said, putting them on. "I was cleaning these when I walked into your big cat here. I suppose that's why I didn't see it."

Barbara and I gazed down at our wrecked creation. I bent to scoop up the two green marbles, which had rolled to my feet.

"I'm Tess Swinhart," she said. "Not that it's a name you'll necessarily want to remember."

That last comment made me laugh a little and I felt my shock fade. Turning to the girl, I took a good look at her.

She was tall, I'd guess at least five feet nine, and big boned, with broad shoulders. She wasn't fat, but she was a very large person. Her hair was light blonde. The thick black frames of her glasses might be the first thing —

the only thing — you noticed about her face. I'd seen her without them, though, so I had a different impression. She had light blue eyes, a slightly upturned nose, and a wide mouth. An unusual face, but not bad looking.

She wore a short, pale pink cardigan buttoned up to the top. It covered a white blouse with a lace-trimmed Peter Pan collar, which peeked over the cardigan. Her pants were loose-fitting brown corduroys. And, as I mentioned, she was wearing black boots. (I couldn't help thinking that she must have been cleaning her glasses when she put that outfit together too. But I quickly pushed that mean thought aside.)

Barbara and I introduced ourselves as we knelt to pick up the remnants of our jaguar. The head had held together, even though it had come off the body. Three of the legs were still intact too.

"I suppose we could stick these back together," Barbara said. "But we'll have to build the whole body frame again. And that was the toughest part."

"I'll put Claudia back on the job," I said, cradling a damp jaguar leg in my arms.

"I'm fairly good at art," Tess said. "I should help you. It's the least I could do."

"I suppose we could use an extra set of

hands," I agreed. "Sure. Come to the cafeteria tomorrow after school."

"All right," she agreed, seeming to feel better. "Is there anything I can do to help right now?"

I glanced at my watch. "You could help Barbara take stuff back to the art room so I can leave," I suggested. I still had a couple of hours until my BSC meeting, but I needed to get home and have something to eat. It's important that I eat at very regular intervals, because I'm diabetic. That means my body has trouble regulating the amount of sugar in my bloodstream. If my blood-sugar level gets too high or too low it can be seriously bad news. So I monitor my blood sugar closely, watch what I eat carefully, and give myself injections of insulin every day. I have to be responsible about doing those things, but it's not a major problem.

"Sure thing," Tess said. "You go ahead."

Barbara smiled and handed her the tub of leftover papier-mâché goo. "You carry this, and I'll bring in the parts," she told Tess. " 'Bye, Stacey. See you tomorrow."

" 'Bye," I said as I headed home. I hoped we'd done the smart thing by allowing Tess to help us fix the jaguar. She did seem a little klutzy; then again, anyone could have an accident. A sudden sharp cry made me look back. "Uh-oh," I murmured.

Tess had bumped into Alan Gray while holding the tub of papier-mâché. She was now frantically wiping the front of Alan's papier-mâché–covered jacket while Alan silently fumed. Barbara looked on, stifling her laughter.

It might not have been funny if Tess had dumped papier-mâché all over someone else, but Alan Gray is one of the most obnoxious boys in our class. He's not just the class clown; he's always playing a prank on someone. In other words, his jokes are often at someone else's expense, and they're not always funny.

This time, though, the laugh — and the papier-mâché — was on him. All over him, in fact. "Way to go, Tess." I giggled. Unintentionally, she'd done something a lot of us have been wanting to do for ages.

I watched as Alan stormed away. He has no sense of humor when it comes to himself. I walked through the gate, feeling worried.

I hoped this accident wasn't going to come back to haunt Tess. Alan Gray on a revenge kick could be pretty unpleasant. He was probably already thinking of pranks to get her back.

I walked into Claudia's bedroom at five-fifteen, in plenty of time for our five-thirty BSC meeting. Claudia was already there, of course. Our BSC president, Kristy Thomas, was there too. I greeted them, then plunked myself down on Claudia's bed, my usual spot. "Bad news," I said to Claudia, then went on to explain about the smashed jaguar.

"What dweeb did that?" Claudia asked.

"That new girl, Tess . . . something," I said, unable to recall her last name.

"Swinhart," Abby Stevenson supplied as she bounded into Claudia's room. "She's in my homeroom. She's so odd."

"Where does she come from?" I asked. "She has kind of a strange way of speaking."

Abby snorted. "Stranger than my Long Island accent?"

"Yes, even stranger than that," I replied with a laugh.

"I know what you mean," Abby said. "I don't know where she's from, though. Maybe she made up that weird way of talking to go with the rest of her weird self."

"Don't you like her?" I asked.

"She's okay, I guess," Abby said, stretching out on the rug. "I don't really know her. No one does."

"She smashed Stacey's jaguar," Claudia told Abby.

"Oh, bummer."

"What's a bummer?" asked Jessi Ramsey as she hurried in and took her regular spot on the carpet. Her best friend, Mallory Pike, came in behind her and sat down next to Jessi.

Before I go any further, I should probably tell you about the BSC and all its members. I'll begin with the club itself.

We call it a club because we're all friends and we love getting together, but the BSC is really more a business than a club. A baby-sitting business, to be exact. A super successful baby-sitting business.

Kristy had the idea for the club one afternoon, back in seventh grade, when her mother couldn't find anyone to sit for Kristy's little brother. Mrs. Thomas was going crazy making a zillion phone calls. It occurred to Kristy that it would be a lot simpler if her mother could call one number and reach several qualified baby-sitters at once.

So, she rounded up her best friend, Mary Anne Spier, plus Claudia, who rounded up *me* (I had just moved to Stoneybrook). She said she wanted to start a baby-sitting business with a group of sitters who would all be available at one number at certain times. And that's exactly what we did. We are the original Baby-sitters Club members.

We spread the word — and Claudia's private phone number — around town, and the calls came pouring in. Over time, we've expanded. We now have seven regular, full-time members and two associate members. Plus one honorary member — Dawn Schafer, a former member, who moved to California.

We meet here in Claudia's bedroom every Monday, Wednesday, and Friday from five-thirty until six. During that time clients call to set up sitting appointments. Whoever is closest to the phone takes the information about the job. Then, we decide who should accept the job, and we call back the client to confirm.

Now I'll tell you who we are. I'll start with me, Stacey McGill. I'm thirteen and in eighth grade (so are most of my BSC friends), and I was born in New York City. I still live in the city — part-time, anyway. My parents are divorced, and I spend some weekends with my father, who stayed there after the divorce. What else can I tell you about myself? I've already mentioned my diabetes. I have blue eyes and shoulder-length blonde hair. I like clothing and fashion and math.

Since I like math, and I'm good at it, I'm the club treasurer. Each week I collect the dues. (Everyone grumbles about paying.) We use the money to replace our supplies, to help pay Claudia's phone bill, and for other expenses. If we find ourselves with surplus funds, we plan a pizza party or something else fun.

Who should come next? My best friend, Claudia. I've already mentioned that she's an artistic genius. She's great at any kind of art. She even brings her artistry to her unique outfits. Jewelry-making, beadwork, tie-dyeing, weaving — all those things go into making Claudia a one-of-a-kind dresser. She looks fantastic in the outfits she creates. That's partly because she's good at putting them together and partly because she's gorgeous. She's Japanese-American and has beautiful, straight black hair, almond-shaped eyes, and perfect skin.

It's amazing that Claudia has perfect skin, since she's a junk food fanatic. Her parents don't approve of junk food, so she stashes the stuff all over her room. Any visitor to Claudia's room is in constant danger of sitting on a concealed bag of potato chips or stepping on a stowed-away Ring-Ding.

The other things Claud hides are her Nancy Drew mysteries. Claudia is a big Nancy Drew fan, but her parents don't think the books are "intellectual" enough. I suppose they're used to the tastes of Claudia's very intellectual sixteen-year-old sister, Janine. She's an actual genius and very studious.

Claudia is *not* studious. School bores her and it shows. Even though she's thirteen, she's repeating the seventh grade because her grades were very poor. (Her spelling is beyond belief.)

Since we use her room and her phone, Claudia is our vice-president. She's also in charge of hospitality. With her love of snacks, she's a natural for the job.

Kristy Thomas is our president. Talk about a natural for a job! She's super organized and energetic — a born leader. She's also down-to-earth, talkative, blunt (sometimes too blunt), and athletic.

Kristy doesn't look especially presidential. At five feet nothing, she's the shortest girl in the eighth grade. And she's not fashion conscious at all. Her long brown hair is unstyled, and she almost always wears jeans and a sweatshirt, turtleneck, or T-shirt. But Kristy really knows how to get things done. She's always coming up with great ideas. We call her the Idea Machine.

One of her great ideas was Kid-Kits. These are boxes — each member has her (or his) own — stocked with fun stuff to bring on baby-sitting jobs: craft materials, markers, joke books, hand-me-down toys. We don't take them on every job. But if we think the kids will be shy, or if they're sick or upset about something, we take them along as an extra cheerer-upper.

Another of Kristy's ideas was the club notebook. In it, we record what's happened on each of our sitting jobs. It's a very handy reference, especially if you're going to sit for a family for the first time, or you haven't seen them for awhile. You can look in the notebook and learn about them from club members who've recently sat at that household.

Kristy's dad ran out on their family back when Kristy's younger brother was a baby. Things were tough for the Thomases, but the Thomases were tougher. Mrs. Thomas remarried. Her new husband is a millionaire named Watson Brewer. When that happened, Kristy and her three brothers (two older, one younger) moved across town to Watson's mansion. Watson's kids from his first marriage, Karen (who's seven) and Andrew (four), live with them part-time. Kristy's grandmother

Nannie lives with them too. She helps take care of two-and-a-half-year-old Emily Michelle, born in Vietnam, whom Watson and Kristy's mother adopted.

Down the street from Kristy lives Abby Stevenson. She's our newest member. She moved here from Long Island, which is just outside New York City.

At first, I wasn't sure how well Abby would fit in as a BSC member. I was worried because she's as forceful as Kristy — just as outspoken, and just as firm in her opinions. In the beginning, the two of them did clash. But I think they've grown to appreciate each other. And Abby has a great, wacky sense of humor that goes a long way toward easing tension. She keeps us laughing.

Abby has a twin sister, Anna. For identical twins, they look pretty different. Both have deep brown eyes and curly, dark brown hair. But Abby wears her hair in a wild mane, while Anna keeps hers short. Both girls have glasses *and* contact lenses, and they both wear whichever they feel like. On any given day, chances are that one is wearing her contacts, while the other has on glasses.

Their personalities are pretty different too. Abby is outgoing and athletic, while Anna is quiet and musical.

The only other member of Abby's immediate

family is her mother, who is an editorial director for a publishing company in New York City. Mr. Stevenson died in a car accident when Abby was only nine.

Abby is our alternate officer, which means she has to be ready to jump into any other officer's job if that member is not at a meeting for some reason.

Our club secretary is Mary Anne Spier, Kristy's best friend. Like Kristy, she's petite, with brown hair and eyes. That's where the comparison ends, though. Mary Anne is quiet, and she's an excellent listener. She's very sensitive — so sensitive, in fact, that she cries easily. She's not particularly interested in clothing, but she has a nice casual style. Her hair is cut short. It's a cute look for her.

When I first met her, Mary Anne didn't seem nearly as grown-up as she does now. That was because her father wouldn't let her be grown-up. Her mother died when Mary Anne was a baby, so Mr. Spier was Mary Anne's only parent. His idea of being a good dad was to be very overprotective and strict about everything, including the way Mary Anne dressed and wore her hair. She looked like a little kid, all the way up to seventh grade.

Mr. Spier began loosening up, though, around the time he married Dawn's mother, Sharon. Dawn (our honorary member, remember?) came to Stoneybrook with her mom and brother, Jeff, after their parents split up. Sharon had grown up in Stoneybrook before moving to California.

Dawn and Mary Anne quickly became friends, and Dawn joined the BSC. One day, they discovered that Sharon had dated Mary Anne's father, Richard, in high school. From that moment on, Dawn and Mary Anne were determined to reunite their parents and become stepsisters. Crazy as that sounds, they did it.

Only, things didn't work out exactly as they had planned. Mary Anne and her dad moved into Dawn's wonderful old farmhouse on Burnt Hill Road, but they discovered that becoming a new family wasn't easy. They worked their way through their problems (issues such as neatness, pets, tastes in food, and privacy). Then, just when things seemed to be running smoothly, Dawn became homesick for California. After going back and forth a few times, she finally decided to live there for good with her dad, his new wife, and Jeff (who had already returned to California).

As you can imagine, Mary Anne was crushed. She's been coping pretty well, though. And you know what? Through all her emotional turmoil, she never made a mistake in the club record book.

As secretary, Mary Anne's in charge of the record book (another of Kristy's great organizational ideas). The record book is like the brain of the BSC. It holds everyone's schedules, keeping track of things such as the weekends when I'll be in the city with Dad, Abby's soccer games, practices for Kristy's Krushers (that's a little-kids' softball team Kristy coaches), Claudia's art lessons, and so on. Every time a client requests a sitter, Mary Anne checks the book to see who is available. When we've decided who'll take the job, Mary Anne records that information in the book. This way there's no misscheduling and everyone receives a fair share of jobs.

The book also contains important facts about our clients — addresses, children's names, rates paid, and any special information such as allergies, anxieties, or unique house rules. Luckily for us, Mary Anne is excellent at keeping track of it all.

Guess what. Mary Anne is the only one of us BSC members to have a steady boyfriend. His name is Logan Bruno, and he's a club member too. Usually, he doesn't come to meetings, but we can call him to take a sitting job if we have more work than we can handle. This makes him an associate member.

Our other associate member is Shannon Kilbourne. She lives in Kristy and Abby's neighborhood. When Dawn left, we asked Shannon to take her place full-time, but Shannon was so busy with activities in school that she couldn't give enough time to the club and the jobs. So she went back to associate status, which works better for her.

Last — but absolutely not least — are our two junior officers, Mallory Pike and Jessica Ramsey. They're both eleven and in the sixth grade. Because of their age, they can't baby-sit at night (unless it's for their own siblings). But the jobs they take in the afternoons free the rest of us to work evenings, so they're invaluable.

They're good sitters too. Maybe it's because each is the oldest child in her family.

Mallory has seven brothers and sisters! She's smart and studious, but she has a witty way of looking at life. She wants to write and illustrate children's books one day. I can easily see her doing that. She says she'll never allow her photo to be shown on her books because she isn't happy with her appearance. She dislikes her reddish-brown curls, her glasses, her nose, and her braces. She doesn't realize that her braces will come off someday, she can wear contacts when she's older, her nose is fine, and her hair is pretty. I bet that by the time she needs photos for a book jacket, she'll have dozens of great ones to offer.

I think we'll be seeing photos of Jessi in print one day too. That's because she's an incredibly talented dancer. She studies ballet and has already performed in several professional productions.

Jessi looks like a dancer. She's lean and graceful. She wears her black hair pulled back from her face the way dancers do. And she dresses like a dancer. Leotards are her trademark.

Jessi's family consists of her mom; her dad; her aunt Cecelia; her younger sister, Becca (eight), and the baby, John Philip Ramsey, Jr., also known as Squirt. (He's not yet two.) The Ramseys moved to Stoneybrook because Jessi's dad was transferred to Stamford (the nearest big city). There aren't very many other African-American families in Stoneybrook, though, and unfortunately, not all of the Ramseys' new neighbors were friendly at first. That was dealt with, though, and now the Ramseys have lots of good friends.

So that's the BSC. At five-thirty, we were assembled in Claudia's room. The conversation I'd begun about Tess was still going. "So what if she's strange," Claudia said. "I'm sure some people think I'm strange because of the way I dress."

"I hate to break this to you, Claudia," Abby said, "but you *are* strange."

Claudia threw a bag of M & Ms at her. "Oh, thanks a lot," she said, laughing.

"Seriously, though," Abby said. "You look like you know what you're doing. Tess looks like she picks her clothes out in the dark, or as if her closet exploded and some of the clothes just happened to land on her."

"So what if she's not into style?" Kristy commented.

"Hey, I'm not saying it makes her a bad person. She's just strange, that's all," Abby replied.

"Speaking of strange," Mallory began, "has anyone noticed that my brother Nicky is acting very strange?" (Nicky is a third-grader.)

"I've noticed," Mary Anne agreed. "Remember when I sat at your house with you last Saturday and Nicky was having secret phone conversations with someone all night? Did you ever find out who he was talking to?"

"Jackie Rodowsky," Mallory told her. "He calls Jackie Rodowsky every second, and they whisper."

"Strange," Mary Anne said, opening the record book. "I wonder what they're up to." She checked the book. "Claudia, you're sitting for the Rodowskys this week."

"I'll see what I can find out," Claudia volunteered as she passed around a bag of popcorn.

"Good," Mallory said. "I'm dying to know."

The next morning, I was at my locker when I looked up and noticed Tess walking down the hall. It would have been impossible not to notice her. She was wearing a hot pink sweat outfit with frilly lace around the collar and sleeves. Her large size, combined with the heavy black-rimmed glasses, made the outfit look . . . wrong. Way wrong.

I could see kids staring at her as she passed, but she seemed happily unaware of their astonished glances. "Hi, Stacey," she greeted me. "I'll see you this afternoon. I have some ideas on how to fix that poor creature I bashed up yesterday."

"Great," I said. "See you then."

Tess walked away and Alan Gray tapped me on the shoulder. "Did she call me a poor creature?" he asked with a smirk.

"Not you, Alan," I replied, closing my locker, "the school mascot Barbara and I were working on yesterday. She accidentally stepped on it."

"Well, she *accidentally* dumped a tub of papier-mâché on my head," he said. "She's a walking menace. A gigantic, neon pink walking menace."

"I saw what happened," I told him. "She didn't dump it on your head. She bumped into you and it spilled. It was just a little accident."

*"Little?"* Alan cried.

"Oh, give me a break, Alan. It looks like you survived the horror."

"Barely," he grumbled.

"It's not like Tess Swinhart was out to get you."

"Swinhart!" he exclaimed. "Is that really her name? It should be Swine-heart! She looks like a huge pig in that pink outfit."

I bit back the smile about to form on my lips. I didn't want to give Alan the satisfaction of laughing at his dumb joke. Lame as it was, though, the joke had a point. Tess did have a slightly upturned nose. And when she was dressed in pink like that . . .

"Swine-heart the Destroyer," Alan rambled on. "Pig on a rampage. She could be a new comic-strip villain, able to turn into a wild boar at will. Swine-heart versus the X-Men. Swine-heart demolishes the Fantastic Four!"

Rolling my eyes, I left Alan at the lockers and walked toward my homeroom. I had no idea what a big mistake I had just made.

Armed with Tess's last name, Alan decided that the idea of Swine-heart the Destroyer was the funniest thing anyone had ever come up with, and he was determined to share it with all of SMS.

The idea spread fast. By second-period Cokie Mason handed me a note to pass to David Gabel, who sat on the other side of me.

The note was folded just once, and I saw the top sentence. It said: "Swine-heart, the Pigpen Years." I flipped it open and saw it was a crudely drawn comic about "The evil Swine-heart as a piglet." The little pig wore glasses like Tess's.

*This isn't funny,* I wrote on the top of the comic and handed it back to Cokie. She made a disgusted face at me. (Cokie and I have never liked each other anyway.) She scratched out my comment and then handed the note to the kid behind me, who passed it to David.

As class went on, David sent the stupid comic on to another kid, who handed it on to another. I was thankful Tess wasn't in the class.

She turned up unexpectedly in my English class, though. "I'd like you all to meet Tess Swinhart," Mr. Fiske said. "She's been reassigned to this class." He turned to Tess. "You can take that empty seat at the end of the aisle."

The seat was behind mine. I smiled at Tess as she sat down. "How come you were transferred?" I whispered, swiveling around in my seat.

"They had put me in remedial English," she replied. "But I don't need that kind of work. I'm fine in regular English."

"Why did they think you needed remedial English?" I asked.

"Because my old school is — "

Mr. Fiske cleared his throat loudly, and I turned around in a hurry. He began his lesson on medieval poets with a poet named Chaucer whom everyone had been wild about back then.

It was *not* my favorite area of English. I could barely understand the way the language was spoken back then. And the poem, called *The Canterbury Tales,* was about different people telling different stories — not exactly fascinating stuff. At least it didn't fascinate me.

"Now, class," Mr. Fiske said toward the end of the period, "you will have two weeks to work on a project that represents some aspect of medieval culture. It may be anything you choose. I want each of you to pick a partner and work in pairs."

I groaned and slumped in my seat. Such torture!

Tess tapped me sharply on the shoulder and

I turned around. "Want to be partners?" she asked.

"I . . . I guess so," I replied.

She smiled broadly and I noticed that she had a small space between her two front teeth. "What about castles?" she said.

"What about them?" I asked.

She made an exasperated face. "For our project! I know a lot about castles. A whole lot. We could build one."

"We could?"

"Sure. Easy."

All I could imagine was building some big castle and Tess accidentally falling on top of it the day it was due. "That sounds good," I said without much enthusiasm. At least she had an idea, which was more than I had.

"Terrific," Tess said. "This is going to be a blast. I adore the Middle Ages."

*She adores the Middle Ages?* Oh, well, everyone's different. I certainly had never met anyone who adored the Middle Ages, though.

"I'll see you at lunch," Tess said, heading for the door.

As she stepped outside, someone in class made a loud oinking sound. I turned to see who'd done it. It was impossible to tell, though. All I could see were the smirking faces of five boys and a couple of girls seated in the far corner of the class.

Barbara, Tess, and I had planned to meet in the lunchroom that afternoon to rebuild our jaguar. I'd tried to talk Claudia into coming, but today was the day of her sitting job at the Rodowskys.

As I neared the cafeteria I saw something that made me stop a moment. Tess was standing outside the doors, talking to Clarence King and some of his pals.

This spelled trouble to me.

Clarence, who insists on being called King, is not my favorite person. (He once gave Logan Bruno a terrible time, just for being a BSC member.) I wondered what he was up to with Tess.

I started walking again, quickly. Tess probably needed my help, and the sooner I reached her, the better.

"I just wanted to welcome you to SMS, Babe," he was saying as I came into hearing distance. He emphasized the word "Babe" and his friends grinned. "I'll be seeing you, *Babe*."

Tess smiled and nodded as they walked away. But I winced. Babe — as in the movie (and book) about the talking pig. I *knew* that was the joke.

"He seems pretty nice," Tess commented.

"Not really," I replied sourly.

She looked confused. "He's not?"

"He called you Babe!"

"I know, it's not politically correct to call someone a babe. That's true," Tess conceded. "I suppose I should tell him not to call me that."

"Definitely. Tell him that." Tess had missed the insult entirely. She had no idea half the school was busy making pig jokes at her expense. And I didn't want to be the one to tell her.

Maybe it would all blow over in a day or so. Maybe she'd never realize what was going on and her feelings wouldn't be hurt. I hoped so, anyway.

"Come on," I said, pushing the swinging door to the cafeteria. "Barbara's probably inside waiting."

I was right. Barbara was there with the pieces of the jaguar spread out on a table. "Hi," she greeted us. "I'll be right back. I'm going to the art room for the other stuff we need."

Tess and I began arranging the pieces. Tess

dug into her backpack and pulled out a large spool of wire mesh. "What's that for?" I asked.

"I was thinking that if we wrapped the frame in the mesh, it would hold together better and not be quite so fragile," she replied. "The papier-mâché would be easier to lay over this wire too. It will have more to cling to."

"Brilliant!" I cried, and I meant it. Even Claudia hadn't thought of that. "Where did you find the mesh?"

"I bought it," she said as she unrolled the stuff. "I bought these wire cutters too. We'll be able to cut it to fit."

"You didn't have to do all that," I said.

"Sure I did." She began cutting a section of mesh. "I wrecked it, didn't I? It's my fault."

"It was an accident," I said.

"Accident is my middle name lately. I don't know what's the matter with me. Suddenly I'm so clumsy."

"It's probably the new place. You don't know where anything is yet." I thought about the easy way I moved around SMS. I knew every turn, every doorway by heart. It took time to feel that familiar in a place, though. I'd moved around from place to place enough to know that. "What was it like at your old school?" I asked.

"Oh, it was great," she replied, looking up from her work. Behind those awful glasses, her eyes were bright. "I had the best friends. We were always doing wacky things. Like, once, in art class, we carved an entire fleet of yellow wooden ducks and set them afloat in the river. You should have seen the boats going crazy trying to avoid them."

I laughed, picturing the scene.

I suddenly felt very sorry for Tess. She wasn't so bad. In fact, she was pretty nice. She just needed some smoothing out. A few fashion tips wouldn't hurt either.

I wondered if I could help. If she didn't look like such an oddball, maybe the kids wouldn't make fun of her.

"Your school was by a river?" I asked.

"Yes, it was one block away from the — "

"I found everything," Barbara called, staggering through the door under a pile of rags, wood, newspapers, papier-mâché powder, and sponges.

"Here, I'll help you." Tess hurried to Barbara's aid.

We spread everything out and set to work. Tess's wire mesh made the job so much easier than it had been the first time around. As we worked, I thought of a subtle way to drop a fashion hint to Tess.

"Barbara, you know my friend Mallory, don't you?" I asked.

"I think so. Yeah," Barbara replied. "She's

that cute sixth-grade girl with the curly hair and glasses."

"Right. Well, she just hates wearing glasses. She's dying for contact lenses. Her parents have always said no. They think she's too young. But it seems like lately they're close to changing their minds. Do you know any good places that sell lenses?"

Actually, I knew where kids went for contact lens prescriptions. I just wanted to work in a hint to Tess. Her looks would improve so much if she ditched those awful glasses.

Barbara named several eye doctors she knew of, plus a couple of places in the mall that did lens fittings. As she spoke, I stole glances at Tess to see if any of this interested her.

It didn't seem to. She was concentrating on wrapping the jaguar's balsa wood rib cage in mesh. It was as if this discussion of contact lenses had absolutely nothing to do with her.

I'd have to try harder. I'd have to be much more direct.

The next day I heard Tess pig jokes everywhere. It was horrible.

In the morning, I passed by a locker on which someone had scrawled, "Hi, Petunia!" I stopped short. It had to be Tess's locker. Who else would be called Petunia? As in Porky Pig's girlfriend, Petunia Pig.

I didn't want Tess to see this.

I ducked into the girls' room across the hall and grabbed a wad of toilet paper. I soaked it, then darted back to Tess's locker. The person had used a washable marker, and the writing faded quickly. But it didn't come off completely.

"Hi," Tess said. I was so busy scrubbing that I hadn't heard her walking down the hall.

"Oh, hi," I said, jumping.

Tess frowned. "Why are you washing my locker?"

I let out a nervous laugh. "Uh, there was some graffiti on it, and I didn't want you to find a messy locker. You know. That can be a bummer. I'm sure it wasn't anything personal. Just . . . one of those things."

Tess peered at the faint, blurred writing that remained on her locker despite my scrubbing. " 'Hi, Petunia'?" she read. " 'Pe*tun*ia'? I guess it was meant for someone named Petunia. I suppose whoever wrote it had the wrong locker."

I looked at her for a moment, not knowing what to say. Maybe she didn't know who Petunia Pig was.

"It was very nice of you to clean my locker, though," Tess continued.

"No problem," I replied as my eyes traveled over her latest outfit. A bright pink, yellow, and red plaid pantsuit. It looked like something I'd seen in old disco movies from the 1970s. I couldn't imagine where she'd even found such a thing.

She realized I was studying her outfit. "Like it?" she asked. "It was my mother's."

"I don't know." I didn't want to be a hypocrite and say I adored it. "It's hard to get used to the style."

"I know." Tess beamed. "That's why I like it so much."

I nodded. "Well . . ." I let my voice trail off.

"Hey, want to come to my house tomorrow afternoon?" Tess asked. "I've got some books on castles. I dug up some photos I have too. We could start on our project."

"I suppose so. Sure."

Tess smiled, then turned to open her locker. " 'Bye," I said, drifting away from her. I took one last look at her in that terrible plaid polyester pantsuit, then walked away.

The wheels in my head turned. Suddenly I had a brilliant idea. Tomorrow I'd be alone with Tess. I could use the opportunity to give Tess a makeover. This girl desperately needed to be saved from herself!

"Hey, Tess," I called to her. She turned toward me. "Do you mind if we work at my house? I . . . uh . . . have a meeting and I can work longer if I'm not too far away." (This happened to be true.)

"Okay," Tess agreed.

I smiled and waved. Great! I had a day to plan Operation Makeover Tess.

Tusedays

mallory is defanately wright. Sumthing is going on with her bruther. He is acting like a secrut ajent on a mishon. Jackie R. is being odd also. Wut culd they be up to?

On Tuesday afternoon, Claudia went to the Rodowskys' house to baby-sit for the three boys — Archie, who's four; Jackie, who's seven; and nine-year-old Shea. She was wearing her oldest overalls. If she could have, she would have sprayed herself with stain repellent. Somehow, sitting for those three always turns into a disaster. It's Jackie who's responsible for most of the mayhem. He doesn't do it on purpose. He just seems to attract, well, disaster. In fact, we refer to Jackie Rodowsky as "the Walking Disaster." He's always falling over something, painting himself, knocking something down, getting stuck inside something, tripping. But we're crazy about him. He and his brothers are adorable and fun. (Shannon thinks Shea has a crush on Claudia.)

When Claudia rang the bell that day, it was answered by the three boys, standing in size order. All three have red hair and freckles. "Hello!" sang Shea.

"Hello," Jackie sang in a higher tone.

He had to nudge Archie, who then yelped out, "Hello!"

Shea shook Archie's shoulder. "That was terrible. It was supposed to be in harmony, Archie!"

Archie stuck his tongue out at Shea.

Claudia laughed. "It sounded good to me."

Suddenly, Jackie lunged forward and looked sharply in both directions. Then he darted back into the house and leaped over the front couch, hiding behind it.

"What's the matter with Jackie?" Claudia asked as she stepped into the front hall. "What's going on?"

"Don't ask," Shea said, waving in the direction of the couch. "He's gone nuts, that's all."

"Nutsy cuckoo! Nutsy cuckoo!" Archie shouted gleefully.

"Gone nuts?" Claudia asked with a smile.

"Wacko," Shea confirmed matter-of-factly. "He's been this way for a week."

Claudia knelt on the couch and peered over the back. She discovered Jackie, whispering on a cordless phone to someone. He realized Claudia was gazing down at him and he looked up with a little smile. "Okay, see you soon," he whispered into the phone, then he clicked off.

"Is something the matter, Jackie?" Claudia asked.

Jackie sprung up. "Not anymore."

"Are you sure?"

"Absolutely. Everything is A-OK. Under control! No problemo!"

"See?" said Shea. "Wacko!"

"Who did you call?" Claudia asked Jackie.

Jackie shrugged. "A friend."

Mrs. Rodowsky came in then, already wearing her jacket. "Hi, Claudia," she said. "I'll be at Washington Mall, and I'll give you the number of my new cellular phone." She dug in her canvas shoulder bag. "I wrote the number down on some masking tape I stuck on the back of the phone. Now where is the phone? I thought I put it right in my purse last night."

"Here it is!" Archie cried. He'd found the phone in Jackie's open backpack, leaning against the closet.

Mrs. Rodowsky shot Jackie a questioning glance. "Why is my cell phone in your backpack? Did you take it to school today?"

Jackie's skin turned so red his freckles seemed to disappear. "I guess so," he admitted in a small voice.

"Why?"

"In case of an emergency?" Jackie ventured feebly.

"Were you expecting any particular type of emergency?" Mrs. Rodowsky asked, taking the phone from Archie.

"A twister!" Jackie cried. Clearly the idea had just occurred to him. "You know, a tornado. I wanted to be able to phone home if a tornado was coming."

"We don't generally get twisters in Connecticut," said Mrs. Rodowsky.

"But it could happen," Jackie insisted. "You never know."

His mother rolled her eyes and laughed lightly. "This phone is not a toy," she told Jackie. "You're not to take it again."

She wrote the number of her cellular phone on a small notepad and left it on the front-hall table for Claudia. "Be good, guys," she said to her sons as she departed.

"Why did you really take Mom's phone?" Shea asked Jackie the moment the door was shut behind his mother.

"I told you," Jackie insisted with an exasperated sigh.

"Yeah. Sure. Like I really believe that," Shea scoffed. "You're lying."

"Am not!"

The brewing argument was cut short by the doorbell. When Claudia opened the door, Nicky Pike was standing there with his arms folded, wearing an extremely serious expression. "Hello, Claudia," he said in what Claudia figured was meant to be a formal, businesslike tone.

"Hello, Nicholas," she replied.

He didn't seem to catch the teasing in her greeting but strode purposefully past her into the living room.

"Wow! You got here fast!" Jackie cried, his voice full of relief. "I thought I saw — " He cut himself short.

"What did you see?" Claudia asked.

"I saw . . . uh . . . that . . . uh . . ." Jackie replied, his eyes darting as he tried to think of something to say. "Uh, that it was nice out and we should go and do something. Something outside." He grabbed Nicky's arm and pulled him toward the back door. "Come on!"

Claudia watched them leave. "Strange," she murmured.

"Want to see my new video game?" Shea asked. "It's really cool. I'll teach you."

Claudia settled down cross-legged in front of the TV as Shea booted up the game. Archie hopped onto her lap. It was a jungle game, with monkeys and tigers and hunters chasing each other. Claudia liked it and found that she was pretty good at it too. But, after her tiger chased a hunter up a tree and she won the first level, she decided it was time to check on Nicky and Jackie. "Be right back," she said, settling Archie on the floor.

She walked to the back window and peered out at the small yard with its big toolshed and half-blue doghouse. (She remembered when the Rodowsky boys decided to paint the doghouse. It had been another messy, disaster-filled day.)

Gazing around the yard, Claudia spotted Nicky and Jackie practicing what looked like some kind of martial arts moves. Everything appeared to be calm, so Claudia returned to the video game. She made it back in time to see Archie's video monkey fall out of a tree. GAME OVER, the screen flashed. "Your turn," Shea told Claudia.

She played until she won the next level, then decided to check the yard again. This time, the scene was less calm: Nicky and Jackie were tottering along the edge of the toolshed roof, waving their arms for balance.

"Uh-oh," she murmured. Jackie the Walking Disaster on top of the toolshed? Visions of a record-breaking disaster flashed into Claudia's head. "I'll be right back!" she called to Archie and Shea as she dashed for the back door.

Bounding into the yard, she stopped and gazed around. The boys weren't on top of the shed roof. They weren't anywhere. They'd disappeared.

"Jackie!" she shouted. "Nicky!"

The only sound was the gentle swoosh of the big pine tree that extended into the Rodowskys' yard from the Segers' yard, on the other side of the fence.

Claudia was confused. It had taken her less than a minute to get from the window to the yard. How could the boys have vanished so quickly? She peered over the fence into the Segers' yard. No one was there.

"Jackie! Nicky!"

Suddenly, Claudia became aware of something falling around her head and shoulders. She reached for the top of her head and pulled a small bunch of pine needles from her hair. Looking up, she saw Nicky and Jackie balancing on the branches of the tree.

"Why didn't you answer me?" she demanded.

"We were practicing invisibility," Nicky explained with deadly seriousness.

"Well, practice visibility and come down from there," said Claudia.

The boys made their way down. Claudia watched them intently, worried that one of them would slip. (Especially since Jackie has fallen from a tree before.) They did fine, though, all the way down onto the toolshed roof. Claudia didn't breathe easily until they were on the ground.

"Who were you hiding from?" she asked them.

The boys exchanged glances. "No one," Nicky answered. "I was just showing Jackie how to disappear in an instant when the enemy approaches. Then you can jump down and take them by surprise."

Claudia gazed up at the tree. "If you had jumped down from there, *you* would have been taken by surprise," she told them. "You'd be plenty surprised when you broke all your bones."

"Naw," Nicky scoffed. "You'd just go into a roll."

"You've been watching too much TV," Claudia told him. "And what enemy are you expecting anyway?"

Again, the boys looked at one another. "Just in case there *was* an enemy," Nicky said.

"Hey, you never know," Jackie added, with what had apparently become his favorite saying.

"That's for sure," Claudia said as she ushered them into the house. She didn't know what was going on with them. But something definitely *was* going on, and she had the feeling it would only be a matter of time before she found out what it was.

On Wednesday after school, I walked with Tess to my house. "My mother works," I explained as I unlocked the front door. "She'll be home by five-thirty. I'll have to leave before then, though. I have a meeting. We can work in the dining room." The night before, I'd equipped the dining room with everything I thought I'd need. A stack of books about hair, makeup, and fashion sat in the middle of the table. My makeup bag was on the hutch behind the table.

Tess took a seat while I went to the kitchen to cut up some carrots and apples for a snack. When I returned with the plate, Tess was already paging through the beauty books. Yes! My plan was working.

"What are all these for?" Tess asked.

"All what?" I replied innocently.

"All these books."

I looked at the books as if I were surprised to

see them. "Oh, the books! They're just some fashion and beauty books I happened to have lying around."

"You don't need them," Tess said. "You look great."

"Thanks. But you can learn new things in these books. I always discover interesting tips." I flipped open the nearest book. "Here, look at this. Did you know that soft curls can soften a too-square or too-round face?"

Tess studied me. "Your face isn't too square or round."

This was going to be harder than I thought. What did it take to get through to this girl? She absolutely could not take a hint.

"I was thinking of cutting my hair," I said (which wasn't true). "You know, just for a change. Do you ever think of growing yours out?"

"No," she replied. "I like it short. It's easy."

Tess turned to her pack and took out some photos. She spread them on the table in front of me. They were all of castles. "We can choose from a lot of different styles," she began. "These aren't all medieval, though. Some are later than that. This one is older. It was originally a Roman fortress that was later added onto when — "

"Tess," I interrupted her. "Why don't I give you a makeover? It would be fun."

"A makeover? Do you think I need one?"

"My friends and I give each other makeovers all the time. We just think it's fun. I have lots of makeup."

"All right. If you want to," Tess agreed, though she sounded uncertain.

"Great."

Tess removed her glasses and I began to work. I used an example I'd found in one of my books as a guide and created a very natural-looking makeup for her.

I worked on Tess for nearly an hour. All the while, I talked about clothing and hair, dropping heavy hints. "I'm applying a lot of makeup," I said. "But I only wear a little to school. You'd look great with mascara and some blush." I figured the mascara might make her eyes show up more behind her glasses, and the blush would give her face a less round (and less piglike) look by adding some shape.

When I was done, Tess stood before the dining room mirror. "What do you think?" I asked.

She squinted and leaned forward. "I can't really see myself without my glasses." She put them on. "Nice, I guess," she said without much enthusiasm.

"Too bad you can't see without your glasses," I commented. "You might like it better. Have you ever thought about getting contacts?"

"I've had them for a couple years now."

"You have?" I gasped. "Why don't you wear them?"

Tess shrugged. "Glasses are easier. Besides, I like them."

Tess always seemed to leave me speechless. She constantly said things I didn't expect.

Glancing at my watch, I saw I would need to get going or I'd be late for my meeting. "Wow! The time's flown," I announced. "Sorry, but I have to leave for my meeting."

"But we didn't even work on the project," Tess protested.

"The project isn't due for awhile," I replied, gathering my things. "Kristy — she's the club president — gets so mad if we're late. And she has a point. We all have to be there to make the club work."

"You certainly are involved in a lot of clubs," Tess commented. I couldn't tell if she thought that was a good thing or a bad thing.

But it gave me an idea.

If kids got to know Tess — and discovered that she was all right — the pig jokes would probably stop, and she'd have the chance to make new friends.

"Why don't you join the Pep Squad?" I suggested.

"I don't know," Tess replied.

"You're already working on the jaguar with

Barbara and me," I pointed out. "You might as well join officially. There's a meeting tomorrow."

"I'm not sure it's my sort of thing."

"Sure it is." This was a great idea. It would make all the difference for Tess. I couldn't let her pass it by. "You don't have to be peppy, you just have to support SMS. Come tomorrow. Check it out for yourself. Barbara will be there. And if the jaguar's dry, we can paint it."

"I suppose so. Okay," Tess agreed, still looking uncertain.

The next day, Thursday, I didn't run into Tess until lunchtime. I was disappointed to see that she wasn't wearing a bit of makeup. "Hi, Tess," I called as she passed by the lunch table where I always sit with my BSC friends (except for Claudia, Jessi, and Mallory, who have lunch at different times).

Tess held her tray in one hand, like a waiter. Everything she did seemed to make her stand out.

Her outfit that day might have been the worst one yet. She wore baggy pink overalls and a long-sleeved, satin shirt with a bright (and I mean *bright*) pattern of pink and green daisies all over it. She had also clipped a small (but bright) pink plastic barrette in her short hair, the kind little kids wear.

"You're coming to the Pep Squad meeting, aren't you?" I asked.

"I'll give it a try," she answered, setting her tray down on the end of our table.

"Good. I'll see you then."

"Okay. See you."

"Why didn't you invite her to sit down?" Kristy asked when Tess was out of earshot.

"I don't know," I replied. "There's no room."

"We could have pulled over a chair," Kristy insisted.

"I don't really know her that well," I said defensively. Now that I thought about it, I should have invited her to sit with us. I looked around the cafeteria. *Oh, good,* I thought. She'd found a seat with Barbara.

"I thought her outfit was sort of cute," Mary Anne commented.

Kristy rolled her eyes. "Are you serious? Well, I suppose there's nothing wrong with being unique."

"Of course not," I said, "but Tess's uniqueness is making her the target of mean jokes."

Abby nodded. "In homeroom this morning, a girl called her Swine-heart right to her face."

"Oh, no!" Mary Anne gasped. "What did she do?"

"She just corrected her. 'It's Swinhart,' she said, calm as anything. I don't think she understood that it was an insult."

"She never gets the insults," I put in, shaking my head in bewilderment. How could she be so unaware of what was going on?

"That's good. Maybe she never will catch on," Mary Anne said hopefully.

"I don't know," said Kristy. "Eventually she's going to realize what's happening."

"That's what I've been trying to say!" I told them. "When she *does* realize, her feelings are going to be hurt. I just want to help her before that happens."

"Then why didn't you ask her to sit down?" Kristy asked again.

"I didn't because I didn't," I snapped, suddenly irritated. "Let's talk about something else."

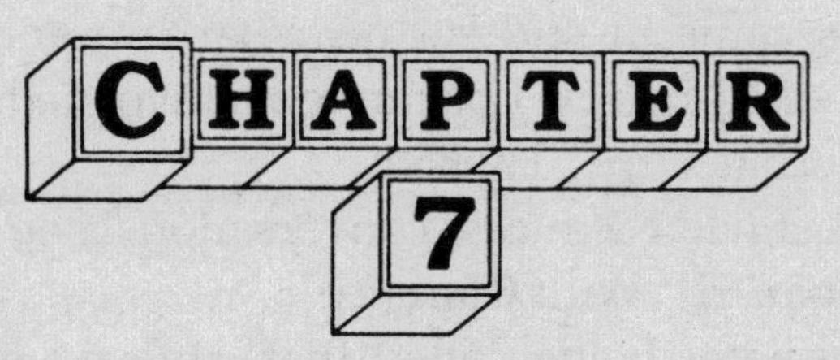


After school that day, I was sitting in the classroom where the Pep Squad meets when Tess came to the door. That idiot Clarence King was talking to her again. She stood in the open doorway listening to him, an interested expression on her face. He wore a rudely smirking smile.

Why didn't he just leave her alone? I really can't understand people who go out of their way to be cruel. I absolutely don't get it.

Barbara slid through the doorway and slipped into the desk behind me. "Is Clarence being nice to Tess?" she asked me.

I shook my head. "He's making fun of her. He keeps calling her *Babe*."

Barbara cringed. "I've been hearing those pig jokes all over school. Someone showed me a Swine-heart the Destroyer comic book today. I think Alan Gray put it together, but now lots of kids are adding strips of their own, like it's an ongoing story."

"Those kids should get a life," I grumbled.

"Definitely."

Tess came in and sat near Barbara and me. She looked happy. I began to feel worried. "Hi, Tess. What's up?" I asked.

"I just had the nicest conversation," she said.

I moaned. "With Clarence?"

"He hates being called that. He said to call him King."

"He would. That guy is in love with himself. It's like that expression — he's a legend in his own mind."

A look of annoyance came over Tess's face. "He doesn't seem so awful. In fact, he seems pretty friendly."

"Clarence? Are you sure?" Barbara asked gently.

"Yes."

"How can you stand being called Babe?" I cried. I was bursting to explain the reference to her, to tell her that it was even more insulting than it seemed. But how could I? To explain about Babe being a movie pig would mean telling her about all the pig jokes. I simply couldn't do it.

"I asked him not to call me that anymore," Tess said. "He promised not to."

"Well . . . good," I said skeptically. I hoped

it was good. On the other hand, if Clarence didn't call her Babe anymore, he might come up with something even worse.

The meeting began. We discussed our first big football game, which was in a couple of days. It was an away game, but buses would be provided.

"I want to make a suggestion," said a boy named Jeff Cummings. "I think we should change the SMS mascot."

"No way!" I cried. "We're almost finished making the jaguar. We've worked really hard on it."

"Change it for next year, then," Jeff replied. "I don't think a jaguar is much fun. We need something better."

"Like what?" asked Erica Blumberg.

"I was thinking of an aardvark," Jeff said.

"Oh, that's tons of fun," said Cokie Mason.

"I don't know. Does anyone else have an idea?" Jeff asked.

"Why don't we take suggestions?" Barbara said. "Everyone write down an idea and pass the papers forward. We'll see how they look." Kids scrambled for paper and began writing immediately.

Personally, I liked the jaguar. If I could be any animal it would be a lion or a panther — and a jaguar was pretty close.

I wrote panther on my paper. I didn't want

to be stubborn about the jaguar. Besides, that way, all we'd have to do next year would be to paint the jaguar black.

I handed my paper to Barbara. "What did you write?" I asked Tess.

"Nothing," Tess said in a disinterested voice.

"Why not?"

"What for? Who cares what the mascot is?" she answered. "Do you care?"

"Well . . ." I considered the question. "Not a lot. It's just part of the fun of the whole thing."

"Different people find different things fun, I suppose," she said.

Barbara sat at her desk and flipped through the suggested responses. Curious, I leaned over her shoulder. The first four were: unicorn, dragon, moose, and raccoon. Someone suggested a Martian. Then Barbara flipped to a paper on which someone had written "Tess."

How mean!

Barbara met my gaze and her eyes flashed angrily.

The next paper said "Swineheart the Destroyer." Barbara quickly flipped past it. Among the other suggestions, Tess's name came up three more times. My eyes darted around the classroom as I tried to figure out who had done this.

Cokie, for sure. And possibly her best friend,

Grace Blume. Todd Long and Brent Jensen were also possibilities. They were pals with Clarence King.

"Read them," Erica Blumberg said.

Barbara read a few, leaving out the ones that said "Tess," of course. She did read "pig," though, and a wave of snickering laughter rippled through the group.

"Well?" Barbara said to the group.

"We should vote on it," Jeff suggested.

"I have an idea," Barbara said. "Why don't we see if everyone in school can vote on it? We could do it during halftime at the game."

There was a general murmur of consent. Everyone seemed to think this was a good idea.

"Speaking of the game, let's go through the fight song we're going to lead," Jeff suggested.

Tess slumped in her desk seat as if this were the most torturous thing she'd ever heard of.

"Come on, it's fun," I said.

Tess just buried her face in her hands. "I thought we were going to work on the jaguar," she mumbled.

"We can do that tomorrow."

Tess groaned loudly.

How was she ever going to make friends if this was her attitude? I couldn't help her if she didn't do anything to help herself.

Jeff turned to me. "Stacey, did you photocopy the words?" I'd volunteered to make the copies at the last meeting.

"They're in my pack," I told him. I took the stack of lyrics from my pack and handed them out, saving the last three sheets for Barbara, Tess, and me. I walked back to them in time to hear Tess telling Barbara about her old school. "I liked it much better than SMS," she said. "The kids were more . . . I don't know how to say it . . . more sophisticated, perhaps. Not so uptight."

Barbara nodded.

I rolled my eyes. Tess didn't seem to have a clue about how to be likable.

Tess didn't even try to sing the fight song. Her bored expression told the world that she wanted no part of what was going on.

At the end of the meeting, Claudia came by. She'd finished with Art Club, and we were going to walk home together. I resolved to try one last time to give Tess a helpful hint, to make her look better and fit in better.

I introduced Claudia to Tess, who smiled quickly.

"What a smile! Tess has the best smile," I said to Claudia. "You really do, Tess. Only no one ever gets to see it. You should smile more. You look so attractive when you smile. Doesn't she, Claudia?"

"Sure, yeah," Claudia agreed, looking uncomfortable.

"Thanks," Tess muttered.

"Well, 'bye," I said to Tess. "See you tomorrow."

Claudia and I began walking toward the doors. "Should we have asked her to walk with us?" Claudia asked.

"No," I said. "She lives in the other direction."

"Uh . . . Stacey . . . don't take offense, but I think you went overboard with that smile business. Why don't you just let her be herself?"

I stopped and faced Claudia. "Because *herself* is a disaster!" I cried. "Kids suggested her as the school mascot! Clarence King is acting as if he's interested in her, but really he's just making fun of her."

"Are you sure?"

"Of course. Kids are making insulting comic books about her. When she finds out what's going on, it'll be horrible. Claudia, the girl needs help. She needs to work on her image if she wants to make friends."

"I suppose, but are you *sure* you're helping her?" Claudia said.

"Positive," I insisted.

Thursday

I have to solve this mystery. Not Knowing what's going on with my brother is driving me crazy. I think he's lost his mind.

Nicky hasn't lost his mind, Mal. But whatever he and Jackie are doing sure is strange.

On Thursday, while I was being frustrated by Tess's lack of pep, Mallory and Jessi sat for the Pike kids. Since there were four kids to watch, we arranged for two sitters. (The triplets, her ten-year-old brothers, weren't there that day.)

Mal's and Jessi's jaws fell open when Nicky strutted down the stairs. His hair was slicked back, and he was wearing sunglasses . . . and sporting enormous biceps muscles under a football jersey. His expression was completely serious — so serious, Mal told me later, that it was funny.

"What happened to you?" Mallory sputtered, trying not to laugh.

He turned to her but didn't answer. Instead, he smoothed back his hair, which shattered Mallory's self-control. She collapsed onto the couch with laughter. "Are you trying to look tough?" she asked when she'd caught her breath.

"I don't look tough, I *am* tough," he growled.

"Oh, come on, Nicky," said Jessi. "What's going on? Are you in a play or something?"

"I never play," he replied. "I always mean business."

"Oh, give me a break!" Mallory cried. She tweaked his muscles and heard the sound of paper rustling. "You're not fooling anyone with those."

Nicky made a face at Mallory just as the phone rang. He lunged across the room for it. "Hello?" He listened and nodded. "Are you on the cellular phone? What is your location at the present time?" More nodding. "I'll meet you there."

"You'll meet who where?" Mallory demanded as Nicky hung up the phone.

"Jackie," he replied, grumpily pulling wads of paper towels from the neck of his shirt. "We're going to play a game of football on the playground with a bunch of kids."

Vanessa Pike, Mallory's nine-year-old sister, came into the room. "Football is fun if you like to run," she sang out. Vanessa wants to be a poet and tries to rhyme everything she says.

"Football!" cried Margo Pike (who's seven) as she came down the stairs. "Who's playing football? I want to play."

"No girls," Nicky told her, scowling. "It's a touch football game."

"No girls? That's silly. Why don't we all go together?" Mallory suggested. "I'll get Claire ready." Claire, who's five, is the youngest Pike.

"Ah, come on," Nicky groaned. "*Claire* isn't going to play, is she?"

"She can watch with Mallory and me," Jessi told him firmly.

Vanessa studied Nicky for a moment. "What's with the shades?" she asked, laughter in her voice. "And the hairdo?"

"Nothing!" Nicky snapped as he stormed out the front door.

"Don't leave without us!" Mallory called after him. She found Claire in the rec room and helped her get ready to go. Together, Jessi and the Pikes hiked over to Stoneybrook Elementary School. Nicky walked ahead of them, trying to pretend he wasn't part of the group. "What *is* his problem?" Mallory said to Jessi.

"Beats me," Jessi replied.

A block from school, Mallory saw a kid's hand dart out from behind a tree and grab Nicky, yanking him back behind the thick trunk. Alarmed, Mallory sprinted ahead.

"All three of them are there," she heard a familiar voice say excitedly. Looking around the tree, she saw Jackie.

"Hi, guys," she said. "What's going on?"

"Nothing," both boys answered at once.

She eyed them skeptically. "All right. Let's go to the game." Jackie and Nicky continued walking ahead of the group. When they reached the school, the game was just starting. Nicky and Jackie ran onto the field, joining the same side.

The rest of the Pike kids, except for Claire and Mallory, joined the game. As Mal and Jessi watched, they slowly became aware of something odd. Nicky never left Jackie's side. Wherever Jackie ran, Nicky ran too.

"What's he doing?" Jessi asked.

Mallory shrugged. She realized that Nicky was being too rough with anyone who came near Jackie, even when Jackie didn't have the ball.

"Hey!" yelled a boy with buzz-cut blond hair. Nicky had pushed him back hard as he ran alongside Jackie.

Now Nicky spread his legs wide and balled his hands into fists. The other boy did the same.

"Hold it!" Mallory shouted. "Time-out!"

The entire game stopped. All the players looked at her as she marched across the grass and grabbed Nicky's arm. "He's sorry," she told the blond boy. Then she steered Nicky off the playing field. "That's not like you," she said. "Why did you push that kid?"

Nicky folded his arms stubbornly. "Because . . . he bugged me." He glanced back at the field, but the blond boy had returned to the game and was no longer paying attention to him.

Mallory knew Nicky wasn't telling the truth, but she tried to remain patient with him. "Tell me what's going on," she said firmly.

"I did," Nicky insisted.

Jackie joined them. He stood there, panting. "That was a close one," he said to Nicky.

"What was a close one?" Mallory asked, completely exasperated now. "I didn't see any close one!"

Nicky and Jackie simply gazed at her with maddening silence. "All right, Nicky. You're sidelined. You're not playing until you tell me what's going on."

Glowering at Mallory, Nicky dropped to the ground and sat there, cross-legged. Jackie did the same.

"You can play, Jackie," Mallory told him. "I can't ground you."

"It's okay," Jackie replied. "I don't want to play without Nicky."

The boys sat out the rest of the game, until Mrs. Rodowsky arrived to pick up Jackie. "See you tomorrow," he told Nicky as he brushed grass from his jeans. "I'll meet you on Slate Street."

"Check," Nicky said.

Mallory watched Jackie run to the Rodowskys' car. She didn't like the feel of whatever was going on. Someone was going to get hurt, and she had the troubling sense it would be Nicky or Jackie.

Hurray, I thought that Friday when I saw Tess coming down the hall. She wasn't in pink, or pink plaid, or pink daisies, or any form of pink whatsoever. She was actually in blue!

Her outfit wasn't too bad either — nice jeans and a dusty-blue sweatshirt. At least her clothing didn't lend itself to more pig jokes. As she came closer to my locker, I saw that she'd spiked her hair and even had on pale, icy pink lipstick.

"Hi! You look great today," I greeted her sincerely.

"I decided to try some of your suggestions," she said, looking slightly embarrassed. "I look okay?"

"Excellent."

She leaned against the locker beside mine, looking as if she wanted to talk about something but didn't know how to start.

"Is something wrong?" I asked.

"Yesterday, as I was leaving the meeting," she began slowly. She hesitated again.

"What?" I said softly.

"Someone oinked at me as I walked by." She spoke quickly now. "At first I thought he just burped or something, but then he did it a second time and it was a definite oink."

I drew in a sharp breath. This was just what I'd been afraid of. "Who was it?"

"A boy. I didn't know his name. Does oinking mean something at this school?"

I opened my mouth to speak, but no words came out. I had no idea what to say.

"I thought maybe it was because I was wearing pink. Could that be it?" she asked. "Is there some unwritten law about what colors are cool? There are so many strange ideas around here about what's cool and what's not."

Once again, she hadn't quite gotten the insult.

"Who knows, with a weirdo like that," I replied. "But maybe pink isn't your best color."

"I love pink," Tess said. She seemed alarmed at the idea that she might not look good in it. "I have so much pink stuff. I like the way I look in pink."

*No kidding*, I thought. "The blue really brings out the blue in your eyes, though," I said, which was true.

"Oh, no, that's probably because I have mascara on," she said. "I hate the way it feels."

"You can't feel mascara."

"I can. My eyes itch and my eyelashes feel sticky."

"How can you feel your eyelashes?" Tess looked so much better with the mascara that I wanted to encourage her to keep wearing it.

She shrugged. "I feel them." Suddenly she pulled herself up straight and paid attention to something down the hall. Following her gaze, I saw Clarence King coming toward us. I glanced back at Tess. She didn't look exactly in love, but she was definitely interested in Clarence.

"Tess," I began, "I don't know if you want to spend time with Clarence. I don't think he's your type." I glanced back down the hall. Clarence had stopped to talk to some of his jerk buddies.

Tess's expression shifted to concern. "Stacey, do you like King yourself? Am I getting in your way?"

"Ew!" I cried. I couldn't help it. The very thought made my skin crawl.

"I think you do," she said. "That explains a lot."

"What?" I cried. "What are you talking about, Tess?"

"Well, you know, I have this feeling that sometimes you're uneasy around me. Are you mad because King seems to like me?"

"Definitely not!" I exclaimed. "I have no interest in him. None. *Nada*. Zilch. Zero. And, I don't think you should either."

"Are you sure? He certainly has an effect on you," she said.

I wanted to scream. This conversation wasn't going the way I had planned. "Believe me, I am not interested in him!"

"All right. If you say so. But you do seem uneasy."

"I have no idea what you're talking about."

Tess studied me for a moment, then nodded. "Okay."

I was glad she'd dropped the subject. But I wasn't about to relax.

I glanced down the hall at Clarence and his friends. I could tell they were talking about Tess. They kept peeking up at her, all of them wearing that awful smirky look.

Clarence left them and headed for us. I shut my locker. "I'll see you later," I said.

The interested expression had come back into Tess's eyes. "All right," she murmured, heading down the hall toward Clarence.

"Remember, we have to finish the jaguar today," I called to her.

She nodded absently.

Clarence stopped to talk to her. He wore a very confident, smug smile. He could tell that

Tess liked the attention he was giving her. And all along he was mocking her.

I couldn't stand to watch it. I turned the hall corner and hurried toward class.

That afternoon, I helped Barbara carry our jaguar from the art room into the cafeteria. He was finally dry and ready to be painted. "It's a shame we probably won't be able to use him next year," I said, setting him down on the lunchroom table.

Barbara nodded but didn't seem too bothered by it. "It was fun making him, though," she said. "I was talking to Mr. Taylor today, and he approved our idea to let the kids vote on a new mascot at halftime during the game tomorrow."

"How would we do it?" I asked. "We can't pass out ballots at the game. Not on such short notice anyway."

"No, that's true. It would probably have to be at the next game then, on Wednesday. That's better anyway, because it's a home game."

Barbara and I opened the jars of paint and spread out newspaper to protect the tabletop. While we worked, we tossed around ideas for ways we could set up the vote.

"I know!" Barbara cried. "We can make big posters showing the different choices, and we'll number them. At halftime we can hold them up, and all the kids would have to do would be to write the number of their choice on a piece of paper. It would be so simple."

"And it would be fun to do during halftime," I agreed. Then I frowned. "Do we have time to make all the posters by next Wednesday?"

"Sure. We have Tess to help us now."

"Do you think we should include the pig choice?" I asked.

Barbara chewed her lower lip as she considered it. "I'm not sure that all the kids who entered the pig were thinking of Tess," she said. "They might just have meant a pig, plain and simple."

"I suppose," I agreed. Although it was hard to imagine any rival school taking us seriously with a pig for a mascot.

"We might call more attention to the problem if we leave out the pig," Barbara added.

"True," I agreed.

Tess walked in just then. Her eyes were bright. "I've got a date!" she sang out. "Next Saturday, King and I are going out to dinner together."

"That's great," Barbara said. "Where are you going?"

"To that new place that's opening in the mall," she replied. "It's called Hog Heaven."

On Saturday morning, Claudia, Mary Anne, and I walked to SMS. (Abby and Kristy were getting a ride from Charlie.) We were going to catch the bus that would take us to the football game at the Sheridan Middle School. Jessi and Mallory were sharing a sitting job, so they couldn't go.

"Tess actually thought *you* liked Clarence King?" Claudia laughed. "Oh, wow!"

"She honestly seemed to believe that I had some problem with her because of it."

"I see what she was getting at. I can't figure out whether you like her or you don't," Mary Anne commented.

"Of *course* I like her. I'm helping her, aren't I?" I replied.

Mary Anne and Claudia exchanged glances. Maybe I had been a little sharp. But I wasn't in the mood to worry about Tess.

Almost the moment we walked through the

back gate, I spotted a tall figure, dressed in vivid pink, moving among the crowd of kids waiting for the bus. It could only be Tess.

"Hi!" She greeted me with a big smile as my friends and I approached. I couldn't believe it. This outfit was the brightest pink yet, and the worst. Bright pink corduroy pants with a boxy, nubby, bright pink sweater. The pink plastic clip was back in her hair and she wasn't wearing any makeup.

My expression must have given away my thoughts. "I'm back to pink again," Tess said, stating the obvious with a smile.

"I see," I replied.

"I just didn't feel like myself yesterday," she explained.

I nodded. Tess was her own worst enemy. The kids would never stop with the pig jokes. Swine-heart the Destroyer would live forever at this rate.

"Barbara and I already brought out the jaguar to put on the bus," Tess told me. "He looks wonderful." She turned to Claudia. "Those green marble eyes are the greatest touch. Stacey says they were your idea."

"Thanks," Claudia replied. "I heard you were a great help in repairing him."

"I was a great help in ruining him in the first place," Tess said with a laugh.

Charlie's car pulled up alongside us. Abby

and Kristy hopped out. "Hi, guys," said Kristy as they joined us.

Two school buses pulled into the parking lot. Kids began forming wide, messy lines as they assembled at each door.

"Tess!" a familiar voice called. I spotted Barbara standing near the farthest bus, the second one to pull in. She was awkwardly holding the jaguar while kids nearby jostled her without meaning to.

"I guess she needs help," said Tess. She wriggled her way through the milling kids toward Barbara.

I started to follow her, but a crowd of kids came between us as they surged toward an arriving bus. I jumped up, trying to locate Tess on the other side of them. She'd reached Barbara and was helping her with the jaguar. They were doing fine without me.

"Come on," Abby called to me. My friends were getting on a bus. I joined them.

The bus ride was a blast. We cheered and sang pep songs. Kids shouted jokes about the Sheridan team. I was glad not to have to worry about Tess or about anyone making pig jokes. I could just relax and have fun.

After we got to the game and found seats in the bleachers, I saw Barbara pass by. Erica Blumberg and Jeff Cummings were helping

Tess with the jaguar. Excellent! I wouldn't have to do a thing.

For the first half of the game, I screamed and cheered along with everyone else in the stands. My friends and I chanted, "Logan! Logan! Logan!" when he ran onto the field. Clarence is on the team too. He scored the first touchdown.

It was a close game. One minute SMS was winning, and the next minute Sheridan took the lead. It was back and forth for the entire first half.

At halftime, the cheerleaders ran onto the field and performed their routines. Then Jeff, Erica, and Barbara carried the jaguar out, while Cokie and Grace led the kids in the stands in the SMS fight song.

I'd hoped Tess would be part of the group holding the jaguar. It would have shown all of SMS that she was a regular kid and not some oddball. When she wasn't there, though, I began searching the bleachers for her.

After several minutes, I spotted her sitting alone on one of the bottom bleachers. The kids next to her were standing, cheering. But Tess was thumbing through a magazine.

Thumbing through a magazine!

Couldn't she at least *pretend* to cheer for the team? After all, Clarence King, her big date, was a player. She could *try* to look like part of the group, couldn't she?

No, not Tess. She had to be the most stubborn person on earth. (The expression *pigheaded* came to mind but I pushed it out guiltily.) She was either stubborn or completely clueless. Whichever, she was determined to do things her own way.

I sighed. Maybe this was my fault. If I'd sat with her at least I could have taken the magazine away and made her stand up and cheer. I had my work cut out for me.

The football game proved one thing to me. Without my help, Tess would never fit in. She'd be eaten alive by the cruel kids who kept making Swine-heart jokes and oinking in her direction.

"Why don't you come to my house today and we can work on the castle," I suggested Monday morning.

Tess looked at me warily.

Why was she angry at me? Was it because I hadn't sat with her? I suppose since I invited her to join the Pep Squad, I should have. Oh, well. I'd make it up to her at the next game.

"Don't you have one of your meetings?" she asked me.

"Not until five-thirty. We could still work until five or so," I replied.

"All right. I've done some work on it on my own. I'll bring it."

"Great!" I said.

I hadn't thought about the castle project for a single second. I hate it when I wind up with a project partner who doesn't do any work. I couldn't believe I was being that kind of partner myself. I didn't mean to be. I just figured we had time.

For the rest of the day, I tried to figure out what I could do to make it look as if I'd done some work on the project. Nothing brilliant occurred to me.

"Give me just one idea," I pleaded with Claudia on the way home from school. "You're creative."

Claudia sighed. "You could glue pebbles to some cardboard to make it look like the outside of a castle," she suggested.

"Perfect," I said. So I walked along, taking a few small rocks from every gravel driveway we passed. I picked up other little pebbles along the way until I had a pocketful.

The moment I came in the door, I grabbed a carrot from the fridge. Then I set to work. I cut up a cardboard box, spread the cardboard on the kitchen table, and began gluing the pebbles to it.

What a mess! The pebbles wouldn't stick no matter what I did. Glue was all over the place. By the time the front doorbell rang, I was covered with glue.

Tess walked inside carrying a large, black

canvas bag. I led her into the kitchen and she stared at my mess. "I have an easier way to do that," she said.

She pulled pieces of white Styrofoam board from her canvas bag. Some kind of pattern was etched into the Styrofoam. The last board she pulled out had the same pattern but had been artfully sponged with different shades of gray paint so that the patterns took on the look of stone. "These can be our walls," she said. "The Styrofoam is easy to cut into whatever shapes we need."

I have to admit, I was very impressed.

"That is excellent," I said. "Where did you get such a great idea?"

"I took a set design class at my old school. We built a huge castle with this stuff for a play. It looked totally real."

"A set design class. Wow! What a great school," I said.

Tess nodded. "Yeah." She took tubes of paint, brushes, and natural sponges from her bag. "I thought we might finish painting these boards together. I'll show you how."

Working on the boards was fun, once I got the hang of it, although Tess's boards came out a thousand times better than mine. "My walls can go in the back," I offered, laughing.

"Maybe so," Tess agreed with a smile.

It was five-fifteen before I even looked at the

clock. "Oh, my gosh! I have to run!" I cried.

We left the boards on the table to dry. Tess packed up the rest of her things. As she did, she asked me questions about the BSC.

"It's great," I told her, "but we don't need any new members. Abby just joined and we're full up."

"I didn't *want* to be a member," Tess said, looking insulted.

"Oh, sorry. I was just telling you since you were asking about the club. I thought maybe you were interested in joining. But there are a lot of other clubs you could join at school. The drama club always needs people to do backstage stuff and the chess club is looking for new kids. Do you play chess? Probably not, right? Me neither. But let's think what else you'd like . . ." I kept talking but I no longer knew what I was saying. It was clear to me, and probably to Tess, that I was just rambling on to cover my embarrassment.

"No problem," Tess said once her bag was packed. "You better hurry. I'll see you tomorrow."

I walked her to the front door and felt miserable as I watched her leave. I sighed. Somehow, I didn't seem to be helping Tess much.

I pulled on my jacket. I felt happy to be going to a BSC meeting. At least there I usually did a good job.

* * *

On Tuesday, Tess's outfit was beyond belief. She was wearing a bright pink blouse with big puffed sleeves over a short black skirt. The skirt was okay. But that blouse! "I was feeling medieval," she explained. "I suppose the castle inspired me."

Inspired her to what? Insanity?

In homeroom, someone passed me one of the Swine-heart the Destroyer comics. I couldn't resist paging through it. The main character was a supervillain pig who was very obviously based on Tess. She wore Tess's big black glasses and that goofy pink barrette in her hair.

Despite feeling bad for Tess, I had to smile at some of the comics. They were pretty funny. Swine-heart the Destroyer would turn into this rampaging boar whenever she got angry and annihilate everything around her.

As each kid added comic squares of his or her own, I noticed a drift away from the super-insulting stuff and a shift toward being more creative. Swine-heart the Destroyer became less evil and more comical. In one strip, she even accidentally helped a superhero named Gray Man (who was undoubtedly begun by Alan Gray) save the world.

There were blank pages toward the back of the book. The first blank said, "Add your comic here and pass it on."

I stuck the book in my pack. At the end of

homeroom I dawdled until almost everyone was gone. Then I went to the front of the class and tossed the Swine-heart book in the trash basket. That good deed made me feel much better for the rest of the day.

After school, I went to the art room to help Barbara finish the posters for the new mascot. A couple of them were especially well-done. "Who did these animal sketches?" I asked.

"Tess," Barbara told me. "We worked on them last night. She's talented, isn't she?"

"She sure is," I agreed.

"Tomorrow at halftime, I'll read the names of the animals on the posters, and you hold up the posters," she suggested.

"All right."

"I asked Tess to read the names," Barbara went on, "but she didn't want to — just like she didn't want to help carry the jaguar at the last game. I have a feeling maybe the Pep Squad isn't for her."

"I have the same feeling."

"You should ask Claudia about getting Tess into Art Club," Barbara said.

"You're right." I didn't really want to get Claudia involved with Tess, though. It would have been like passing my problem over to her, and that didn't seem fair. If I thought some more, I was sure I could think of *something* for Tess to join.

At the Wednesday football game, I was determined to be extra nice to Tess. I complimented her poster sketches, which Barbara had handed to me, tied together with a string, before the game began.

I even sat with Tess, down near the field at the end of a row, and told her who all the players were.

"Is King a good player?" she asked.

"I guess he is," I admitted. "That hard head has to be good for something."

Clarence was the only part of football that interested Tess. The rest of it was obviously boring to her. I pretended not to notice, though.

By halftime, the score was tied. Before the cheerleaders came out, Barbara and I were scheduled to present our possible new mascots to the SMS kids.

"Time to go," I said to Tess. I picked up the posters and slid them under my arm. I walked out onto the field. Barbara was already there, facing the bleachers. She talked into a hand-held microphone, explaining to the kids that they'd have all week to submit the new mascot they'd chosen to any member of the Pep Squad.

"If you want to keep the jaguar, you can submit a ballot saying so," she concluded.

"I nominate Mr. Peter's hairpiece!" some boy yelled from the back of the bleachers. Everyone laughed. I hoped Mr. Peter, who is a math teacher, wasn't there.

"Very funny," Barbara said dryly. "Now, here are the real choices." She began reading the list.

"Eagle," she read. I raised Tess's beautiful color sketch of an eagle over my head. My friends yelled, "Go, Stacey!" I smiled.

"Bear," Barbara said next.

I held up a picture someone else had drawn of a bear.

Each time Barbara read a choice and I held up a poster, some kids clapped and other kids booed. The booers and the clappers shouted funny insults at one another. Maybe it was the excitement of the tied score.

Barbara read "pig," and I drew in a nervous breath as I turned over the poster. I hoped no one would yell out anything about Tess.

The crowd burst into peals of laughter. For a second I thought it was just the idea of a pig for a mascot. Encouraged by the laughter, I held the poster even higher.

But then I glanced at Barbara's horrified face. She was staring at my card. I turned the card around so I could see it.

Oh, no! I dropped it facedown on the ground.

Someone had taken a photo of Tess, blown it up, and pasted it to the poster.

"Swine-heart the Destroyer!" someone shouted. A chant rose up among the crowd. "Swine-heart! Swine-heart! Swine-heart!"

My eyes went to Tess. She was bright red and looked confused.

From somewhere near the top of the stands, someone threw a hot dog at her. The mustard smeared across her jacket. Another hot dog followed, hurtling through the air.

Tess raised her arm and ducked to avoid it. She staggered back, then toppled backward off the bleacher.

A horrified gasp swept the stands. Dropping the rest of my posters, I ran to Tess, but a crowd had already formed around her.

Mr. De Young, a gym teacher, dropped down from an upper bleacher to reach Tess. "Everybody move back," he roared at the kids.

They stepped back, and I was knocked back with them. I had to see Tess. Was she all right?

Wiggling through the kids standing on the

bleachers, I climbed higher up, to where I could see down into the middle of the circle of kids. Mr. De Young knelt beside Tess.

Tears streamed down Tess's face as she gripped her ankle.

Kristy climbed up beside me and looked down. "Oh, wow, she broke something," she murmured. She turned to me. "How did that card get there, Stacey?"

"I have no idea," I replied, feeling like crying myself. "It wasn't there yesterday afternoon."

An ambulance siren screamed in the distance. Within minutes, the white-and-red truck with its flashing red light had raced onto the field.

Mrs. Rosenauer, another gym teacher, ran to the two medics who leaped from the truck. She hurried them toward the bleachers.

"Make way," she commanded the kids.

"I think her ankle's broken," Mr. De Young told the medics. "Her wrist might be fractured too. I'm not sure."

Kristy turned to me and cringed. "Her ankle and her wrist. Oh, that must hurt."

I nodded. I had the horrible feeling this was all my fault, even though I'd had nothing to do with it. I'd never have held up that poster if I'd known what was on it.

I hoped Tess knew that.

What if she thought I'd done it on purpose? That I was in on it?

The medics lifted Tess onto a stretcher and carried her toward the ambulance. I scrambled down the bleachers, desperate to talk to her before they took her to the hospital.

I raced across the grass. "Tess," I shouted, breathlessly. "Tess!"

I reached her just as they were lifting her into the ambulance. "Tess, I'm so sorry," I cried. "Believe me. I didn't know anything about that. I had no idea!"

Tess turned her head away from me.

"You need to leave, miss," said one of the medics. "We have to get her to the hospital."

"I'll come," I volunteered.

"I'm going," Mrs. Rosenauer told me as she climbed into the back. "Why don't you call her parents? Are you a friend of hers? Do you know her number?"

"I'm a friend, but I don't know the number," I replied. I turned to Tess. "What's your phone number?"

Tess turned her head back to me sharply. "Just go away, Stacey," she said in a pain-filled voice. "You're not my friend."

I felt hugely guilty about what had happened, even though I hadn't done anything.

Why was I feeling like this? I wouldn't have held up the poster if I'd known Tess's photo was there.

"Stacey, stop being so hard on yourself. You know the truth," Claudia said to me on the phone that evening.

"Well, then, why do I feel like a creep?" I asked.

There was silence on the other end. Was Claudia considering the question, or was she working up the nerve to say something she wasn't sure I'd like?

"What?" I said anxiously.

"Could it be," she began slowly. "I mean . . . I don't know . . . this is just an idea . . . it's probably not even true."

"Just say it!" I cried.

"All right. . . . Maybe you feel bad about

the way you've treated Tess in general, even though you didn't know about the poster."

"That's crazy! I've done everything I could to help Tess. You know that."

"I know. I know. I didn't say you *should* feel guilty. I just meant it might be why you *are* feeling guilty."

"That doesn't make much sense," I replied. "I'll see you in school. 'Bye."

That evening I couldn't stop thinking about Tess, even when I slept. I dreamed I was pushing Tess off a castle tower.

The next day, just as homeroom began, Barbara and I were called to the principal's office. Mr. Taylor was very upset. I could tell he was ready to let us have it.

Barbara and I told him we had no idea who had changed the poster. At first, he didn't believe it. Slowly, though, we convinced him. We had to tell him what had been going on over the past week or so, with the Swine-heart jokes.

"Tess's ankle is broken and her wrist is sprained," he told us. "She's absent today, and her parents aren't sure when she'll be back. Frankly, they told me she never wants to come back."

"I can't blame her," Barbara said.

"Neither can I," Mr. Taylor agreed. "This kind of cruelty always shocks and bewilders me," he said. "What motivates it?"

"I have no idea," I told him sincerely.

By the time we were dismissed from Mr. Taylor's office, I had only minutes before my first class started, and I had to hurry to my locker. On my way, I met Cokie as she came out of the girls' room.

She smiled at me in a knowing — and extremely annoying — way. I just looked away. She wasn't going to let me ignore her, though. "I didn't think you had it in you," she said as I passed her.

I whirled around. "Had what in me?"

"Oh, come on. You know what I'm talking about."

"I had nothing to do with that!" I said angrily.

"Yeah. Sure."

"I didn't!"

"Oh, relax. It was funny," she said.

"It wasn't funny."

"I guess not, if you have no sense of humor." Cokie strolled away down the hall.

She left me standing there, stunned. How could she be so cold?

I reached my locker and pulled out the books I needed. The halls were nearly empty. As I slammed the door shut, Emily Bernstein came hurrying around the corner. When she saw me, she skidded to a stop.

She clutched my arm. "Don't you feel awful?" she said.

"I didn't have anything to do with it!" I cried.

"I know," Emily said. "You would never do something like that."

I was relieved. I hoped other kids knew that too.

I walked into class just as the PA system crackled to life. Mr. Taylor's voice came on. "I'd like to address the school today in regard to the offensive treatment of a fellow SMS student at the football game yesterday. Rarely have I been so embarrassed by the actions of a student or students as I was yesterday."

He went on, reading us the riot act. I wondered if we'd find out who planted Tess's picture on the pig poster. The photo looked as if it had been snapped in a hall at school, without Tess even being aware of it. Anyone could have taken it. My suspicions were with Alan Gray, Clarence King, or one of their pals in the Pep Squad such as Brent Jensen or Todd Long. Maybe it had been all of them.

At lunchtime I saw Barbara again. "I feel so guilty," I said. "Don't you?"

"No. Why should I?"

"Well . . . no reason . . . we shouldn't," I said. "But I do anyway. You don't?"

She shook her head. "I feel terrible for Tess, but I don't feel guilty. We didn't mean for that to happen."

Then why did I feel guilty?

"I called Tess last night, and she sounded really out of it. She was in a lot of pain," Barbara said. "She sounded depressed too. I told her you and I were as shocked as she was."

"You did? Good," I said. "So, she understands?"

"She understands that we didn't do it," Barbara said. "She doesn't understand why it happened."

"Neither do I." But maybe, in a way, I did understand. Tess had made herself an oddball. And, a lot of times, oddballs become targets.

Tess didn't return to school on Friday. All weekend, I meant to call her, but I kept putting it off. I kept remembering that she'd said I wasn't her friend. Of course, she'd been hurt and upset at the time. Still, I didn't look forward to hearing any more angry words from her.

On Monday, I spotted her hobbling on crutches toward her locker. Her right leg was in a cast and her left wrist was wrapped in ace bandages. "Tess," I said, rushing to her, "how are you feeling?"

"Never better," she replied sarcastically.

"Mr. Taylor gave us a huge lecture," I told her.

She smiled grimly. "Gee, that should make me even more popular."

"Don't feel that way," I pleaded. "Some jerk, or a couple of jerks, did that. Not the whole school."

"The whole school seemed to think it was hilarious," she snapped.

"That's not true." I paused. "I guess you couldn't go on your date last Saturday, could you?"

"No. I had to postpone it until Saturday." Tess studied me for a moment. "Stacey, please leave me alone," she said in a flat, tired voice. "I'd just like to be alone. All right?"

"Okay. But if you need anything, or want to talk, or whatever . . . I'm here."

Tess laughed scornfully. "Yeah. I'll keep that in mind."

I left her alone for the rest of the day. I noticed, though, that kids were being especially nice to her — the nice kids were, anyway. Some held doors for her, and others helped her at her locker.

At lunch, she sat down alone, but I saw several kids stop by to talk to her. On my way to return my tray I headed over to her to say hi, but she angled herself away from me and I couldn't make any eye contact, so I just kept walking.

As I glanced back at her, I saw Barbara sit down next to her. It looked as though they were talking pleasantly.

Tess wasn't mad at Barbara! Then why was she angry at me? If she believed I didn't have anything to do with it what was the problem?

This question drove me so crazy that after my BSC meeting that afternoon, I walked over to Tess's house instead of going home.

When I rang the bell, it was answered by a tall, elegant woman. Her pale blonde hair was swept up into a French twist. There was a very strong resemblance. It was obvious she was Tess's mother.

"Hi, I'm Stacey McGill," I began, feeling very uncomfortable. Had Tess said anything to her mother about me? "I wanted to . . . uh . . . discuss our English project with Tess."

Her mother nodded. "Come in. Tess is in her room. I'd rather not have her come down the stairs again. It isn't easy with the cast. Would you mind just going up? Her bedroom is to the right of the staircase."

"Okay," I said as I climbed the stairs.

"Tess, dear," her mother called up to her. "Stacey is here."

I knocked on Tess's door and she called for

me to come in. "Hi," I said, pushing open the door.

I stood completely still. Tess's room was amazing. A large mobile of colorful, swirling geometric shapes hung from her ceiling. A huge print of a woman, painted by the French artist Matisse, covered one wall.

One side of the room was taken up by a large antique desk. On the opposite side stood her double bed, which was covered in various animal prints. Even the gauzy, see-through curtains at the windows were in a lizard-skin pattern.

It was a great-looking room. I'd never have guessed it belonged to Tess.

Tess sat propped up among her jungle prints. "Hi," she said dully.

"What a great mobile," I said.

"Thanks. It's a replica of a Calder. I got it at the Pompidou Center."

"A what from the what?" I asked with an embarrassed laugh. I'd never heard of either.

"Alexander Calder, the artist. He made a lot of mobiles like that one," Tess explained. "They were showing his work at the Musée National d'Art Moderne at the Pompidou Center. My art group used to go there all the time."

"It sounds French," I said.

Tess laughed shortly. "I hope so. It's in Paris."

"Paris!" I gasped. Almost as the words came from my mouth, my eyes swept across a pile of opened letters lying on Tess's desk. The envelopes all seemed to have the letters "USA" below the regular address. With a closer look, I realized the return addresses were in France.

"Did you go to school in Paris?" I asked, astonished by this discovery.

"Yes. My mother is with the U.S. foreign service. She's a translator for diplomats. And my father works for a French-based perfume company. There are some photos on the desk of my friends and me in front of my old school."

*Paris*, I thought, impressed. Growing up in Paris seemed to me even more sophisticated than growing up — as I had — in New York City. It also explained why Tess might not have understood all the jokes about Petunia Pig and *Babe*. She'd grown up away from American culture.

Turning, I picked up a small stack of photos next to the letters. The top photo showed a smiling Tess, with four of her girlfriends, standing in front of a stone building.

All of them were dressed in pink.

Two of them were wearing black-framed glasses like the ones Tess wore. And another girl had fixed her hair like Tess's. Every one of them wore an outfit I'd consider awful.

But, as I flipped through the other photos, I

saw different friends, and all of them were wearing a similar style.

I suddenly realized that Tess's strange look was *the* look in the school she'd just come from. In fact, on her desk, among the letters, was a French magazine. On the cover was a gorgeous model . . . in a shiny vinyl hot pink pantsuit, short blonde hair, and black-framed glasses.

So many styles started in Paris. In a matter of months, everyone at SMS might be trying to look like Tess!

"Why are you here, Stacey?" Tess asked bluntly, breaking into my thoughts. "If you're worried about our project, don't be. Mr. Fiske gave us an extension."

"I wasn't worried. I came because I wanted to see how you are."

"I'm fine. Now you can go," she said.

"Why are you so angry at me, Tess? I haven't done anything to you. Aren't we friends?"

"Give me a break. You've never wanted to be my friend. All you've done is pity me. I'm not a person who needs pity, Stacey. No thanks."

I felt my face getting hot. Was it from anger or embarrassment?

"I knew kids were making fun, and I wanted to protect you from that," I said. "Is that so bad?"

"No. But you never wanted to know me otherwise. You only just now found out I used to live in Paris because we've never once had a normal conversation. All you do is drop your little improvement hints. You've never talked to me — or listened to me."

"I have too!" I protested.

"No, you haven't. You don't even want to be seen with me. Like I said the other day, you're not my friend."

I drew in a sharp breath. I couldn't argue. The things she was saying were true, and we both knew it. I'd been so busy trying to improve Tess that I'd never even given her a chance to talk. When she tried to, I didn't listen.

"I think you better go," Tess said stiffly. "I'm sure someone could use your pity. But it isn't me."

Tuesday

The case of "Are Nicky Pike and Jackie Bodowsky Losing Their minds?" is finally solved. The answer is — no. They were crazy to begin with! Thank heavens this nuttiness is over. I never would have expected it to end the way it did, though.

On Tuesday afternoon, Abby sat for the Rodowskys. Shea was at a friend's house, so she had only Jackie and Archie to look after. Within minutes of Mrs. Rodowsky's departure, Jackie was frantically phoning Nicky Pike.

Abby watched as the color drained from his face. "What's the matter?" she asked.

Jackie replied in a small, terrified voice, "He's not home."

"So? Invite someone else over."

Jackie shook his head and flopped onto the couch. "This is . . . this is . . . bad," he mumbled, appearing stunned.

Abby sat next to him. Archie ambled in and climbed onto the couch beside her. "What's going on?" she asked.

Archie poked Abby's arm. "Jackie is scared that — "

Jackie lunged across Abby and swatted at Archie. "Be quiet! Be quiet!"

As Abby struggled to pull Jackie away from Archie, the front doorbell rang. "Excuse me!" Abby told the boys. "I have to answer the door."

When she opened it, she found three boys standing there. "Is Jackie here?" asked one of them. (Abby didn't know it, but he was the boy with the blond buzz cut that Nicky had almost fought with at the touch football game.)

"Hey, Jackie, your problem is solved," she said, turning back toward the couch. "These guys want to . . ." Her voice trailed off when she realized Jackie wasn't there. "Where'd he go?" she asked Archie.

Archie pointed toward the back window. "He went to the yard to be invisible."

Abby turned back to the boys. They'd disappeared too. "There seems to be a lot of this invisible stuff going around," she noted wryly, shutting the door.

With Archie beside her, Abby hurried to the back window. She gasped softly at the sight of Jackie teetering unsteadily on the toolshed roof.

She remembered reading Claudia's entry in the club notebook and made the connection. Jackie was going up the tree to practice invisibility.

In the next instant, the three boys appeared in the yard. A look of complete panic swept across Jackie's face. He squinted up at the tree. It was too late. He hadn't scrambled up the branches in time.

The boys glared up at Jackie, who stood, looking stranded and scared, on the roof. Their combative body language told Abby they were ready to fight.

She leaned so close to the windowpane that her nose nearly touched it. If necessary, she was ready to fly out there and protect Jackie. But some instinct told her to wait and watch. She watched as Jackie spoke to the boys from the roof, then crept to the edge and let his legs dangle over. An angry exchange of words was going on between Jackie and the boys.

As the confrontation continued, Jackie climbed down to the ground. He spread his legs wide and didn't look scared. He seemed to be making his points firmly. It appeared to Abby that he was holding his own. He didn't need any help.

"Come on, let's play a game," she suggested to Archie as she walked away from the window. "How about Hungry, Hungry Hippos?"

"Yea," Archie cheered, running to find the game. "Will Jackie be all right?" he asked as he returned with the box in his hands.

"Yeah," Abby said, but Archie's question had made her uneasy. She pictured having to explain a black eye to Mrs. Rodowsky. Suddenly, she wasn't so sure she'd been smart to leave him. "I'll just check," she told Archie as she headed for the back door.

When she stepped into the yard, the boys were still facing one another, looking angry, but not *as* angry. "Is everything all right out here?" Abby asked.

The three boys gazed at her warily. Their faces were flushed with anger. They looked at

Jackie and then back at Abby, waiting to see what would happen next.

"Yeah, everything's okay," Jackie told her. "We had a misunderstanding, but I'm explaining to them what really happened."

Abby nodded. "Okay. It looks to me as if you guys are working this out." She turned and went back inside.

Archie was waiting for her inside the door. "Are they going to hit Jackie?" he asked. "I got boxing gloves for my birthday. Want me to go find them? I could help."

Abby smiled and ruffled his red hair. "No thanks, Archie. Jackie's trying to use words instead of fists. That's always the better way."

Abby and Archie returned to the back window, standing off to the side so they couldn't be seen. Abby smiled to herself at the sight of Jackie shaking hands with the three boys. "Way to go," she murmured. She looked down at Archie. "You should be proud of your brother. He talked his way through whatever mess he was in. He used his head."

Archie nodded. "Can we go back to Hungry, Hungry Hippos now?"

"Sure." Abby and Archie played the game for about fifteen minutes, then Abby heard the back door open. "Is everything okay?" she called to Jackie.

"Yeah!"

Abby decided to check anyway. "Be right back," she told Archie. She found Jackie in the kitchen taking a bag of chocolate chip cookies from the cabinet. He was beaming. "These are for the guys and me," Jackie explained, holding up the cookies. "We've been playing soccer and we're hungry."

"What happened out there?" she asked.

"Those guys thought I stole a jacket from one of them, a baseball jacket," he explained, ripping open the cookie bag. "I told them I have one just like it, but they didn't believe it was really mine. So they said they were going to get me."

"Get you?" Abby repeated. "As in, beat you up?"

Jackie nodded.

It was suddenly clear to Abby. "So you asked Nicky Pike to be your bodyguard?"

"But today I didn't even need him," Jackie said, throwing his arms wide (and sending some cookies onto the floor). "I convinced them it was really my jacket. I told them I got it when my dad took me to a Yankees game, and I described the game and the stadium and everything. I knew so much about it that they finally believed me."

"Good going," Abby congratulated him.

"Wait until I tell Nicky," Jackie said. "I hope

he doesn't mind not being my bodyguard anymore. I think he liked that job."

"Don't worry about Nicky. He'll get over it. If he wants to continue being a bodyguard I'm sure he'll find other kids to protect."

"I hope so, because I don't need him anymore," Jackie said proudly. "I guess I really didn't need him all along."

"I guess not," Abby agreed. Jackie seemed so sure of himself now, she couldn't imagine him ever needing a bodyguard again.

On Wednesday at lunchtime, Emily hurried over to me the moment I came through the door. "I have to talk to you," she said, pulling me over into a corner.

"What's wrong?"

"This morning I was in the newspaper office and I overheard Jim Poirier talking to Alan Gray. I was sitting behind one of the computers, and they didn't see me."

"What were they doing there?" I asked.

"Jim started working on the paper this year. Mostly he writes sports stories, but all the sports assignments were given to other people this month, so I assigned him to write a piece on Hog Heaven, that new restaurant."

She went on to explain that Jim, Alan, and Clarence were planning to play another major prank on Tess. Clarence would take her to the restaurant, where Alan Gray would be lurking with his camera. Clarence would steer Tess near some of the pig decorations in the restaurant, and, secretly, Alan would snap photos. Then, Alan would give the photos to Jim, who would submit them along with his story on Hog Heaven. The pictures would be printed with a lot of snide pig captions, all jokes at Tess's expense.

"But you read all the copy before it's printed," I said to Emily. "You could take it out."

"They thought of that," Emily replied. "They plan to intercept the copy early in the morning, before I send it to the printer, and stick in their stuff. I doubt they'd be able to pull it off, but isn't it a rotten plan?"

"Completely rotten," I agreed. "Not only will Tess be mortified again but she really thinks Clarence likes her. She'll be hurt too."

"Someone has to tell her," Emily said. "I figured since you're her friend, you should be the one."

"We're not really friends," I protested.

"I've seen you two together."

"I know but . . . we're not friends." And it was too bad. Tess probably would have made a cool friend.

Emily frowned. "Well, you know her and I don't. Tell her. Please."

"Okay. I'll figure something out. Thanks for letting me know."

As usual, I ran my problem by my friends. At our BSC meeting that afternoon, we discussed the situation. "Any ideas?" I asked, looking specifically at Kristy, the Idea Machine.

"I do have something in mind," she said thoughtfully.

Everyone turned expectantly to Kristy.

"We'll have to talk to Tess about this, of course. But, if she agrees, here's what we could do . . ."

Kristy laid out her plan. We all loved it.

Looking around the lunchroom the next day, I spotted Tess sitting with Barbara and several of Barbara's friends. I felt so excited by Kristy's plan that I ran to her, pushing her angry words from the other day to the back of my mind. She had a right to be angry with me, but this might begin to make it up to her.

At the table, I said hi to everyone and then asked to speak to Tess privately. She looked at me warily but pushed up onto her crutches and walked away with me.

As tactfully as I could manage, I told her what Emily had told me. I waited for her reaction before continuing. "I'm not really surprised," Tess said bitterly. "When King didn't call to see how I was feeling after the fall, I suspected he wasn't sincere."

I bit down on the urge to say I told you so.

"I'll cancel the date," Tess said. "Thanks for telling me."

"You could cancel," I agreed. "But Kristy came up with a great payback plan that you might like."

When I told Tess about Kristy's idea, she grinned. "Let's do it!" she cried. "Definitely!"

On Saturday, around supper time, Claudia, Abby, Kristy, Mary Anne, and I were camped out on a bench at the mall, not far from the newly opened Hog Heaven. A big pink wooden pig stood at the front entrance.

On her lap, Claudia balanced a plate of French fries that she'd bought at the food court. She used her teeth to tear open her tenth packet of ketchup and squeezed the red goo in swirls onto the already ketchup-soaked fries. "This should do," she said, finally satisfied that she had enough ketchup.

"There's Alan," Mary Anne said suddenly. We looked sharply to the Hog Heaven entrance in time to see Alan Gray enter.

"Is everybody ready?" asked Kristy.

"Ready," we replied.

"Here come Tess and Clarence," Kristy hissed. "Okay, let's go."

I peeked into the garbage bag I held and made sure everything was ready. It was.

We strolled toward the front of the restaurant. (We were all so excited it was hard not to race there.) "Tess!" I called, waving. "Hi!"

A shifty, cornered expression instantly came over Clarence's face. But what could he do? He *was* cornered. He slapped on an uneasy smile and stopped. "Hi," he mumbled.

"Hi, everybody," Tess said with a little too much cheer. "What are you all doing here?"

"Oh, we're just hanging out," Claudia replied, stepping closer to Tess and Clarence.

"Yeah, just hanging," Abby echoed. She stayed close to Claudia.

"Hey, Claud," I said. "Let me have a fry."

Claudia extended her plate to me and I picked a fry from it. "Want a fry?" Claudia offered Clarence and Tess.

Clarence declined. "No, we're going in to eat."

"Go ahead, have one," Claudia urged him, shoving the plate at him. "Oops!"

Claudia pretended to stumble — and smeared the plate of ketchup and fries on Clarence. With one swipe, she slimed his cheek, his chin, and the entire front of his shirt, which was exposed beneath his open jacket.

"Oh," I cried. "What a mess! Let me wipe you off!" In a flash, I produced a rag soaked in blue paint from my plastic bag. Before Clarence knew what was happening, I was wiping blue paint all over him.

He cried out and pulled away from me, stumbling toward Tess. She skillfully leaned back on one crutch and, with her free hand, crowned him with a wreath of whipped cream from the can she'd hidden in her pocket.

"Tess!" Clarence exclaimed.

"Oh, what a shame, King," Tess said sweetly. "I suppose we can't go on our date now."

Clarence stood seething, wiping at his face, which only made the mess worse.

"Sorry, *Clarence,*" she continued. "You'll have to find some other porky Babe to date."

"You girls are going to be sor — " Clarence bellowed.

"No, we won't," Abby said, stepping forward and holding up her camera. "I have a whole roll of pictures of you looking, well, like a pig."

"So unless you agree to leave Tess and the rest of us alone, you'll see these pictures featured in the next issue of the school paper," Kristy said with a smile.

"I write for the school paper too," Claudia reminded him.

"And Emily Bernstein likes *us,*" Mary Anne added.

"So what?" Clarence grumbled, but he knew we had him.

Just then, Alan Gray poked his head out the door. The stunned expression on his face made us crack up.

"That goes for you too, Alan," I said. "Leave Tess alone or I'll tell Mr. Taylor you were responsible for what happened at the game."

"You can't prove it," he said. (Which convinced me that he was the ringleader.)

"Yes, I can," I said convincingly.

"Okay, it's a deal," Clarence mumbled. "Now give me the film."

Abby laughed. "How dumb do I look? We're keeping these pictures as our guarantee. Don't mess with us, and no one will ever see them. But if you do, I'll have them blown up and I, personally, will hang them all over school after they appear in the paper."

"I think we need some ice cream now to celebrate," Claudia suggested.

The boys fumed, red-faced, but there was nothing they could do.

"Come on, Tess," I said. "You must be starving."

"You're right, I am," Tess agreed, and she joined us. We walked away from Alan and Clarence, laughing and talking happily.

When we arrived at Friendly's, we crowded together into one booth. I felt so happy, I didn't even mind having to order a salad while everyone else pigged out (if you'll pardon the expression) on ice cream.

Tess, too, appeared to be truly happy. My friends seemed to enjoy talking with Tess, especially Claudia, who eagerly questioned her about taking art classes in Paris.

"Who wants to shop?" I asked as we paid the bill.

"I can't," Tess said. "I told Barbara and some kids I'd meet them at the movies."

"You and Barbara are becoming good friends," I noted.

"Yeah, it seems that way," Tess agreed. It made sense. Barbara had lost her best friend when Amelia died. And Tess had lost all her friends when she moved. They both needed new friends. They needed each other.

I realized too, that from the start, Barbara had accepted Tess as she is. She hadn't tried to make her over. She hadn't tried to be her bodyguard or her adviser. She just took the time to listen to and learn about Tess.

Which was something I hadn't done.

Outside Friendly's, Tess thanked us again and headed for the elevator that would take her to the movie theatres on the fourth level. "She's an interesting person," Claudia commented as we watched her leave.

"She is," I agreed, "if you take the time to notice."

Claudia gave me a meaningful look. I think she understood what I meant, and how I was feeling about my experience with Tess.

She understood without my saying it because she knows me so well. Which — after all — is what being friends is all about.

Dear Reader,

In *Stacey's Secret Friend*, Tess Swinhart is the new kid at school and has trouble fitting in. At one time or another, you have probably felt that you don't fit in, whether it's in school, in your neighborhood, or even in your family. It's a common feeling. However, when Stacey realizes what Tess is going through, she goes overboard trying to change Tess to *make* her fit in, which ultimately is a disaster.

When I was in seventh grade, I felt much more like Tess than like Stacey. I wanted very much to be a part of the group of "cool" kids in my grade. But as I got older, I realized that they weren't the right friends for me. We had little in common. I soon became close friends with kids who were more like me. If I had tried to change myself — to force myself to be like the other kids — it probably would have been a disaster, just like Stacey's efforts with Tess were. The "real you" (whoever that might be!) is always more interesting and likable than an "artificial you."

Happy Reading,

Ann M Martin

L. GODWIN

# Ann M. Martin

# About the Author

Ann Matthews Martin was born on August 12, 1955. She grew up in Princeton, NJ, with her parents and her younger sister, Jane.

Although Ann used to be a teacher and then an editor of children's books, she's now a full-time writer. She gets the ideas for her books from many different places. Some are based on personal experiences. Others are based on childhood memories and feelings. Many are written about contemporary problems or events.

All of Ann's characters, even the members of the Baby-sitters Club, are made up. (So is Stoneybrook.) But many of her characters are based on real people. Sometimes Ann names her characters after people she knows, other times she chooses names she likes.

In addition to the Baby-sitters Club books, Ann Martin has written many other books for children. Her favorite is *Ten Kids, No Pets* because she loves big families and she loves animals. Her favorite Baby-sitters Club book is *Kristy's Big Day*. (By the way, Kristy is her favorite baby-sitter!)

Ann M. Martin now lives in New York with her cats, Gussie and Woody. Her hobbies are reading, sewing, and needlework — especially making clothes for children.

# Notebook Pages

This Baby-sitters Club book belongs to ______________.

I am __________ years old and in the ______________

grade.

The name of my school is ______________.

I got this BSC book from ______________.

I started reading it on ______________ and

finished reading it on ______________.

The place where I read most of this book is ______________.

My favorite part was when ______________.

If I could change anything in the story, it might be the part when

______________.

My favorite character in the Baby-sitters Club is ______________.

The BSC member I am most like is ______________

because ______________.

If I could write a Baby-sitters Club book it would be about ____

______________.

## #111 Stacey's Secret Friend

In *Stacey's Secret Friend,* Stacey tries to make Tess change the way she dresses and acts. In the end, Stacey realizes she was wrong to do this; Tess is fine just being herself. I felt forced to change once when ______________________________________________

______________________________. This is what I did: ____________

______________________________________________________________

________. Here is how I feel about the way Stacey treats Tess: ____

______________________________________________________________

______________. If I were Stacey, I would have ______________

______________________________________________________________

_______. Stacey is surprised when she discovers that Tess went to school in Paris. A surprising fact about me is ______________

______________________________________. A surprising fact about my best friend is ____________________________

____________________________________.

# STACEY'S

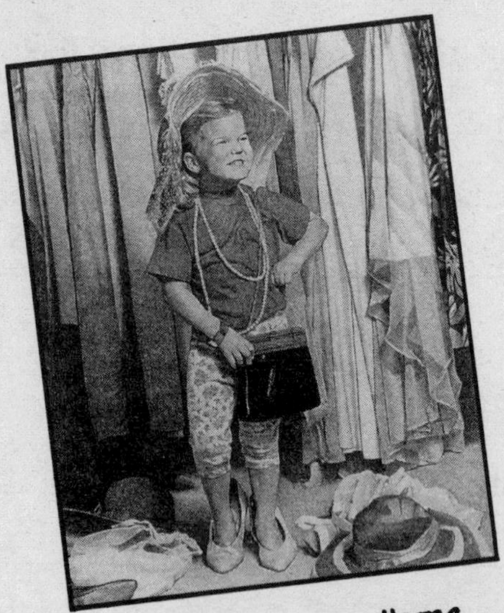

Here I am, age three.

Me with Charl
my "almo

A family portrait — me
with my parents.

# SCRAPBOOK

anssen,
ter."

Getting ready for school.

In LUV at Shadow Lake.

Illustrations by Angelo Tillery

Read all the books
about **Stacey**
in the Baby-sitters Club series
by Ann M. Martin

#3 *The Truth About Stacey*
Stacey's different . . . and it's harder on her than anyone knows.

#8 *Boy-Crazy Stacey*
Who needs baby-sitting when there are boys around!

#13 *Good-bye Stacey, Good-bye*
How do you say good-bye to your very best friend?

#18 *Stacey's Mistake*
Stacey has never been so wrong in her life!

#28 *Welcome Back, Stacey!*
Stacey's moving again . . . back to Stoneybrook!

#35 *Stacey and the Mystery of Stoneybrook*
Stacey discovers a *haunted house* in Stoneybrook!

#43 *Stacey's Emergency*
The Baby-sitters are so worried. Something's wrong with Stacey.

#51 *Stacey's Ex-Best Friend*
Is Stacey's old friend Laine super mature or just a super snob?

#58 *Stacey's Choice*
Stacey's parents are both depending on her. But how can she choose between them . . . again?

#65 *Stacey's Big Crush*
Stacey's in LUV . . . with her twenty-two-year-old teacher!

#70 *Stacey and the Cheerleaders*
Stacey becomes part of the "in" crowd when she tries out for the cheerleading team.

#76 *Stacey's Lie*
When Stacey tells one lie it turns to another, then another, then another . . .

#83 *Stacey vs. the BSC*
Is Stacey outgrowing the BSC?

#87 *Stacey and the Bad Girls*
With friends like these, who needs enemies?

#94 *Stacey McGill, Super Sitter*
It's a bird . . . it's a plane . . . it's a super sitter!

#99 *Stacey's Broken Heart*
Who will pick up the pieces?

#105 *Stacey the Math Whiz*
Stacey + Math = Big Excitement!

#111 *Stacey's Secret Friend*
Stacey doesn't want anyone to know that Tess is her friend.

*Mysteries:*

#1 *Stacey and the Missing Ring*
Stacey has to find that ring — or business is over for the Baby-sitters Club!

#10 *Stacey and the Mystery Money*
Who would give Stacey counterfeit money?

#14 *Stacey and the Mystery at the Mall*
Shoplifting, burglaries — mysterious things are going on at the Washington Mall!

#18 *Stacey and the Mystery at the Empty House*
Stacey enjoys house-sitting for the Johanssens — until she thinks someone's hiding out in the house.

#22 *Stacey and the Haunted Masquerade*
This is one dance that Stacey will *never* forget!

#29 *Stacey and the Fashion Victim*
Modeling can be deadly.

Look for #112

KRISTY AND THE SISTER WAR

By the time I returned to the Kilbourne home, I discovered that war had broken out.

War?

That's right. A Sister War. Declared by Tiffany and Maria. The enemy? Shannon, of course.

I saw the document they'd drawn up, soon after the room-cleaning disaster of a few days before.

*DECLARATION OF WAR*

*We, the undersigned, do hereby declare war on our sister Shannon. We swear to do everything in our power to make her life miserable. The reason for this war is that Shannon is a Big Meanie.*

*signed, Maria Kilbourne*
*Tiffany Kilbourne*

The declaration of war was bad enough, but I nearly lost it when I saw the battle plans they'd drawn up. Like Operation SOS, it was in list form. But this time, the list wasn't full of lovely, sisterly acts. This time it included every nasty prank, obnoxious trick, and diabolical deed two little girls could possibly think up.

They really were going to make Shannon's life miserable.

And there was nothing I could do to stop them.

I tried, believe me. I told them their war wouldn't work if what they wanted was Shannon's attention and love. I told them it wasn't nice to treat their sister that way. And I told them I would do everything I could to make sure they didn't wage war during the times I was sitting for them.

They didn't care. They'd declared war and they were sticking with it. And I was on hand to see the very first battle.